COPPER CANYON

COPPER CANYON

EDWARD N. TODD

DOUBLEDAY & COMPANY, INC.

GARDEN CITY, NEW YORK

1974

For Cella

All of the characters in this book are fictitious and any resemblance to actual persons, living or dead, is purely coincidental.

Library of Congress Cataloging in Publication Data

Todd, Edward N
   Copper Canyon.

   I. Title.
PZ4.T6346Co [PS3570.O38]   813'.5'4
ISBN 0-385-09898-7
Library of Congress Catalog Card Number 74–7637

First edition

CHAPTER ONE

"Thirty, thirty-five, forty 'n even," the wiry little man muttered, dropping the eighth five-dollar gold piece into the outstretched hand before him. "Tom, I still say it's a crying shame you ain't going back home with us."

"Not all that much to go back to," Tom Harrison replied, funneling the gold pieces into a small buckskin bag and snugging up the drawstring. He hefted the bag before stuffing it into a pocket of his jacket; the eight gold pieces rested among many more of their fellows and made a satisfying sound as he tossed the bag lightly. "There's not that much future down there and you know it, at least not for right now. Besides, I've got to make sure that Fergie gets a chance to see the elephant —or at least where he's made some tracks!"

Henry Grayling nodded and turned to the gangling youth beside Harrison. He began counting out eight more gold pieces, dropping them one at a time into the lad's big-knuckled hand.

"Fergie, I had my doubts about paying you grown-up wages when we started combing that brush down there," he said when he had completed the count, "but I don't mind saying that I was wrong. Course, I might'a knowed that any son of Jim Harrison's would be worth his salt and more. There you be, Fergie, 'n damned good luck to the both of you."

Fergie Harrison started to pocket his wages, easily the largest amount of money he had ever held in his hand at one time, but then remembered the gaping holes in both pockets of his baggy, tattered woolen pants. They were the last pair he owned and, like the linsey-woolsey shirt covering his broadshouldered back, had been made by his mother. Instead he handed the coins over to his uncle, who added them to the buckskin bag. They shook hands with Grayling and his two sons and then swung into their saddles.

"Leave some of that north country for us!" Herman Grayling called out as they wheeled away. "Me 'n Calvin, we might decide to strike out thataway in a year or two!"·

Fergie grinned at the squat, thick-chested twins, only a year younger than himself, before touching a spur to his roan gelding. He could see the open envy on their square, earnest faces, so much alike that he could not always tell them apart, even though he had known them for most of his seventeen years, and he suddenly felt much more important.

"You reckon that Herman's ever going to get up north?" he asked when he had jogged up beside his uncle. "Him or Calvin, either one?"

"You can't never tell about such things," came the reply. "They might make it next year. But I reckon old Henry'd kick up right smart of a fuss about that. He figures them boys of his are worth a heap."

"Reminds me of an old mother hen, the way he clucks around them." Fergie chuckled.

He knotted his reins together and draped them loosely over his saddlehorn, as his uncle had done; both shifted about in their saddles, trying to find a more comfortable position as they gave their horses free rein.

Both of them were above average height, approaching six feet, and both had the same broad-shouldered build. Tom's black hair and dark brown eyes contrasted sharply with Fergie's sun-bleached mop of blond hair and light blue eyes. Both of them carried a generous coating of south Texas dust on their worn clothing.

"But then it might come on them just like it did us," Tom continued. "This time next year, old Henry might be laying dead of a fever, just like the one that done in your mammy and daddy. Or Calvin and Herman, they might get it instead —you can't never tell about such things."

Fergie looked away at the mention of his mother and father. Jim Harrison had managed to keep his ranch on the Nueces going during the Civil War, though he had worked almost day and night to do so. Ruth, his wife, had helped as much as she could, as did young Fergie, but the effort had taken its toll. Weakened by the constant exertion and worry, Harrison had stayed out too long in a blue norther that had come whipping down from the Panhandle one February morning in 1865; he had contracted pneumonia and died soon after taking to his bed. Later in the spring a virulent fever had leap-frogged its way along the ranches fronting the Nueces. Ruth Harrison had succumbed to the fever and had died in March.

Tom Harrison, who had been captured while serving with Sterling Price's cavalry in Arkansas in 1862, returned from an Illinois prison camp in July, 1865, to find the Triple H on its last legs. The death of his brother and sister-in-law, together with the lack of a local market for cattle, had been enough to decide him against continuing the struggle. Acting as Fergie's guardian—the youth had inherited his parents' two-thirds of the ranch—he had agreed to lease the acreage to Henry Gray-ling, their closest neighbor. He and Fergie intended to take advantage of the ambitious attempts to trail Texas longhorns into Missouri; they expected to take a job with a herd and collect some hard cash for their efforts, as well as gathering experience for a possible future drive of their own.

"Uncle Tom, you reckon there's really somebody aiming to drive these critters all the way to . . . where was that place?"

"Missouri. A town called Sedalia," Tom replied. "How many times I got to tell you that? Now, as to whether any-body's really going to do it, you figure it out for yourself. We just drove up a little over three hundred head, didn't we? And you know how many other herds we saw or heard about headed up this way, not to count them that's already here. Fergie, there just ain't that many people in San Antonio, so those cattle have got to be headed for somewhere else."

"There's sure a powerful lot of cattle around, that's a fact," Fergie agreed. "What's it like up there, huh? We likely to see any snow?"

"Not this late, you dumb Texan! Now come January, Feb-ruary, along in there, snow might be piled up belly-deep to a big studhorse but not in the summer. Oh, there'll be so many trees you won't know what to think about it all. And not a mesquite tree anywhere! No prickly pear or cholla either. And damp, too—it's mighty damp up that way."

Fergie had spent more than one evening looking at the map in the geography book—one of the four books adorning Ruth Harrison's china cupboard—and still could not fully comprehend the map's scale, which had shown the United States as of the book's publication date, 1849. His uncle had shown him the general location of the Triple H ranch—a difficult task, since almost all of Texas could be hidden under one of the teacups Jim Harrison had once bought from a ship's captain in Indianola—and also marked with his knife the spot where, he thought, Sedalia would be located.

"Here's where we are on the Nueces," he would say when Fergie had brought him the book. "Now if it's that far from here to the coast, you can see it's a devil of a lot farther to Missouri."

Despite his close attention to his uncle's geography lessons, Fergie Harrison still had no real conception of the distance from the Triple H to Sedalia, just as he had no clear notion of a land covered with trees that had leaves as large as his hand but no thorns. He had accompanied his uncle to Laredo the previous October, where they had ridden to buy a wagon and a load of supplies for the winter; that journey—a round trip of about 120 miles—had marked the first time he could remember having been more than a day's ride from the four-room adobe house in which he had grown up.

He had been born in Indianola, on Matagorda Bay, on April Fool's Day, 1849, but his father had waited only a week before leading their two wagons, their four hundred head of cattle, their string of horses and the three oxcarts westward to the ranch he intended establishing. Fergie had no memories of any land but their vaguely defined spread on the middle Nueces River.

"There she is, boy—that's San Antonio," Tom said as they topped a low rise and looked down a gentle slope into a broad plain.

A straggling collection of buildings, some of adobe and

more of the native limestone, together with a prominent few of new, raw wood, sprawled out before them. A line of trees, thick and green, wandered off to the north and south along either side of the San Antonio River. Plumes of dust rose up at different spots to the north of them; one was near enough for Fergie to make out the pack of galloping riders beneath it. Faint whoops of exultation drifted from the riders.

"They must be from that big herd we seen off to the north of where we stopped," Tom remarked. "Yep, they just can't wait to get into town and start spending their wages. Look out, town, there's some wild ones getting ready to howl!"

Fergie nudged his horse forward, and his uncle laughed at the youth's involuntary gesture of eagerness. He touched a spur to the rangy sorrel he was riding, tugged at the lead rope to their packhorse and followed his nephew.

"You reckon there's some of them real bad men in town right now?" Fergie asked as they jogged toward the houses. "Some real, sure enough *pistoleros?*"

"There's bound to be some of that sort there," Tom mused. "You seen how that cattle buyer paid off in gold, didn't you? And all them other herds, they must have been bought with hard coin too. You can figure on it, Fergie: whenever there's gold around, there's bound to be a few people around trying to get some of it for themselves. And without working for it, I mean. You'd best not go flashing your poke around, else somebody just might see if they couldn't get hold of it the easy way."

"I'd like to see anybody try it!" the youth snorted. "I'd bust him good!"

"Hell, boy, there's people around here that could empty your pockets so quick it wouldn't do to talk about it and you wouldn't never feel a blessed thing. Pickpockets, or dips, they call them. I mind this little Irishman I knowed up there in that Rock Island prison camp; he could clean your pockets out and you wouldn't even know he'd been close to you!"

"What'd he want to do that for?"

"He used to make his living that way."

"Huh? You mean he just lived by stealing from people?"

"He claimed he did, back there in New Orleans or wherever it was he come from," Tom assured his unbelieving nephew. "I can believe it too. You just mention work and he'd start looking queasy and getting pale. I guess he'd have fainted dead away if anybody had ever showed him a pick or a shovel. He used to show off for us sometimes, said everybody ought to know how to take care of his money in case he ever went to a big city. But he was slick, I can promise you that!"

"You reckon there's people like that in San Antonio?"

"Why not? There's money there. And it ain't just little Irishmen who're wise to those tricks, either. Girls, some of them, are pretty slick at that kind of work. You know, dance-hall girls and saloon girls."

Fergie had never been in a dance hall and had only the sketchiest knowledge of saloons, much less of the girls who worked in them. He again expressed his astonishment at the ways of a world he had never encountered. He found it especially hard to believe that girls would act in so unladylike a manner.

"Hell, Fergie, what do you reckon them girls are there for? Saloons and gambling halls and dance halls, most of them, they ain't out for nothing but separating you from your money. And girls can help do the job a lot quicker. Most of them, they'd as soon empty your pocket as look at you and they ain't too particular, some of them, about how they do it, neither. Fergie, there's a lot of people in this old world, all sorts of people. Most of them are bad and a lot of them ain't nothing like anything you ever seen down there on that old Nueces!"

"Well, there's one thing for sure," Fergie observed after they had jogged in silence for a minute or two. "Anybody that tries picking *my* pocket, he won't get but a handful of nothing. I reckon the first thing I got to do when we get into town is to get me some new clothes."

"We're both looking a little ragged," his uncle agreed. "Some new clothes might make us look almost decent. That, along with a visit to a barbershop and a bathhouse."

Like his nephew, his trousers sported a rich collection of

patches and snags. His boots, worn and dusty, gaped along the soles. Both of them had hats made the old-fashioned way; a piece of wet rawhide had been positioned over a hole in the ground, hopefully of the same size as the prospective wearer's head, and a rounded log had been jammed into the hole to shape the crown. When the rawhide had dried it had a more or less hatlike appearance, and thousands of cowboys and frontiersmen had worn them. Tom's horsehide coat, cut full in the skirts and equipped with plenty of pockets, was the most elegant piece of clothing on either of them.

Fergie looked closely at the houses that were growing thicker on each side of the broad, dusty road. He soon realized that the women hanging out washing or hoeing their gardens, paying no attention to the riders who passed in front of their homes, were no different from his mother or Eufemia Garza, the wife of the Triple H's foreman. They clumped over a broad wooden bridge spanning the river and were soon in the heart of town. The bridge, broad enough to allow two wagons to pass, seemed huge to Fergie.

"Which way to Mendoza's stable?" Tom asked a man tooling a four-horse wagon loaded with kegs of beer.

"Straight ahead for about a quarter of a mile," the drayman replied in a broad Irish accent. "It's on your left; you'll be smelling it a while before you get to it, never fear!"

Henry Grayling and his sons had agreed to drive the Harrisons' four extra horses, together with their own string, into San Antonio when they had finished turning the herd over to the buyer. Grayling intended to sell off his string of cow ponies, and Rafael Mendoza's stable would serve as a convenient place to show the animals and bargain with prospective buyers, should Mendoza not buy them himself.

"Say, are we going to sell our string too?" Fergie suddenly asked.

"Let's wait and see. Some of them drovers, they might feel more like paying top wages if we could furnish some of our own horses."

"I sure hope we don't have to sell all of them. Old Turnip, here, I'd purely hate to get rid of him, even if he does bite sometimes. And Chino and Mosca, they're good horses too. That Chino, I believe I could cut quail out of a flock with him."

Selling their horses, Tom realized, would cut another of the few ties the youth now had with his home on the Nueces. Those ties were already fragile enough: apart from the clothes on his back and the horses, Fergie's only other tangible connections with home were his father's mesquite-handled army Colt—carried in a saddle holster in front of his right knee—a Spencer carbine, also a legacy from his father, his father's gold-plated watch and a locket which had belonged to his mother. The locket opened to reveal miniature portraits of his parents. They had had the miniatures painted by an artist in Indianola while they were waiting for his mother to gather enough strength to set out on the trek to the Nueces.

"Most likely we'll be able to keep the horses," Tom suggested. "There's hardly any outfit that wouldn't want two good hands with three horses apiece."

CHAPTER TWO

San Fernando Cathedral's bells tolled eleven as Tom Harrison led his gangling nephew onto Military Plaza for the first time ever. A hostler at Mendoza's stable had taken their horses and showed them a convenient corner in which they could stack their saddles, pack and other gear. They had declined with thanks his offer to let them sleep beside their belongings for an extra ten cents a night; they had long ago agreed that they would treat themselves to the luxury of sleeping for at least a couple of nights in a genuine bed, one with clean sheets if such could be had.

"An outfit of new clothes, you say?" Tom asked, surveying his tattered nephew. "Well, I reckon a month of digging long-horns out of that brush down there could make a feller a mite gamey. I notice that people downwind of us are looking a little peaked. Come on, Fergie, let's start getting rid of some of our money."

Fergie kept only his belt and vest, both of which he had made himself, using for the latter the hide of a cougar he had shot two years before, from the outfit he had worn on the drive up from the south. Tom kept his broad leather belt with the brass buckle stamped CSA, together with the big leather jacket. After carrying their purchases to a nearby barbershop and using all its facilities, they again strode out onto bustling Military Plaza, but in a much more resplendent manner. Tom silently noted the fact that, for the first time in his memory, Fergie had not complained about bathing.

"Whoo-eee, they sure do dab on the stinkum!" the youth marveled.

"There wouldn't nobody take us for bankers," his uncle observed, "but I reckon we won't get thrown out of too many places either. Speaking of bankers, we might ought to go over and leave some of our coin in a safe."

They sought out the banking establishment of H. Groos and Company, whose reputation had already spread down to the Nueces, and arranged for a deposit of most of their gold. They had rounded up fifty-three head of Triple H steers, all prime three-year-olds, and had sold them for six dollars each to the same buyer who had taken Grayling's beef. After leaving the bank they sought out the Cattlemen's Rest Hotel, another establishment of which they had heard, and selected as good a room as they could afford. They left their extra clothing there and returned to the plaza, the heart of the city.

"Lordy, fifty cents a day just to sleep there!" Fergie moaned when they were well away from the hotel. "Can't a body do anything in this here place without it costing him some money?"

"He can breathe, maybe, but that's about all."

"I wonder who we'll tie on with?" Fergie mused after they had walked halfway around the crowded plaza.

"There's no need to get all antsy about signing on with just anybody," Tom cautioned when Fergie again voiced his curiosity about which herd they would join for the coming drive to the north. "You seen all them herds out there on that holding ground, didn't you?"

"I sure did," Fergie vowed. "Lordy, I didn't know there was that many cattle in the whole world! Why, there must have been fifteen hundred, two thousand head in some of them herds!"

"There was easy that many in some," Tom agreed. "Well, you can figure that there'll be fifteen, maybe twenty cowboys for every one of them herds. All them outfits we saw, they only had six or eight hands, just enough to hold them right where they were. So they're all going to be wanting hands. Let's just hold it steady for a while, boy, and see about things. Some of them crews are bound to be better than some others. So let's us try to hook up with a good one, huh?"

"I reckon so," Fergie muttered but then, added frowning, "But cattle are cattle, ain't they?"

"Sure they are. But all cooks ain't the same, and I reckon some men would be a sight better to work for than some others. The way I see it, we might pay some attention to things like that. And for another thing, it might be a good idea to throw in with a feller who'd been up the trail before, if there's anybody like that around."

Fergie could not argue with his uncle's reasoning, especially after he had mentioned the widely varying quality of cow-camp cooks. His uncle had often teased him that he did two men's work but ate enough for three, a remark that came close to the truth; for all his appetite, however, Fergie Harrison remained a skinny, rawboned hunk of growing boy. After discussing some of the more memorable cooks they had known, they decided to test the city's restaurants and selected the first establishment they found.

"We sure won't be able to go on like this much longer," the youth grumbled when they emerged from the café, having put away a sizable midday meal. "Two bits that little dab cost me! They sure don't give you much for your money!"

"We ought to put you in a boardinghouse," Tom mused. "One of them places that serves family style, where you can eat till it's all gone. But I reckon any landlady worth her salt would know better than to take you on as a boarder!"

Fergie grinned and followed his uncle out onto the plaza, where they found an empty bench under one of the huge live-oak trees dotting the area. A bewildering variety of men and women passed back and forth before their eyes. Blue-clad soldiers, tangible evidence of nearby Fort Sam Houston, wandered over the dusty plaza; they clung together in tight little knots, neither causing trouble nor attracting it. Businessmen, clerks, housewives and cowboys mingled together in what appeared to Fergie to be a mad, mindless confusion.

Brown faces were every bit as plentiful as white, the youth noticed, and he heard at least as much Spanish as English, as well as occasional snatches of what he took to be Indian tongues. Some of the Indians wore leggings, together with a long shirt and a folded blanket hung over a shoulder; others had adapted to the extent of wearing white men's clothing. A swarm of ragged children darted over the plaza, some offering to shine shoes or run errands and others displaying a wide variety of objects for sale.

After circling the plaza twice, stopping here and there to exchange words with cowboys, Tom led his nephew back to Mendoza's stable. Then they dug into their gear and brought out their pistols, which they unloaded and thrust into their belts.

"You really think it's the best thing, getting these converted?" Fergie asked as they walked away from the stable.

"It makes a lot of sense," Tom assured him. "Everybody says them new brass cartridges is just jim-dandies; not hardly a one ever misfires. And it can rain all day without bothering them a bit. You don't have to worry about a spark getting into your cartridge pouch either, not with them."

"I reckon they'd be some easier to load up, too."

Fergie had once tried reloading his father's percussion Colt while galloping after a wolf; the paper cartridges, each charge wrapped in a cylinder of paper, had been difficult enough to extract from his belt pouch and fit into the chambers while galloping, but the balls had been even harder to seat and the caps had proved nearly impossible to get placed on their nipples.

"They've got to be easier to load," his uncle agreed. "All the time I spent in the cavalry, I never seen but one man who could reload at a gallop and even he'd lose as many caps as he got stuck on. Besides, it took him so long that a one-armed Comanche with eye problems could make him look like a porcupine before he could ever get another shot off, once he'd emptied his piece. No, if we got up there in Comanche country and had ourselves strung out in a running fight, we'd do a sight better, I reckon, if we had our pistols right up to snuff."

They found a gunsmith in a little shop off the plaza who agreed to convert their percussion army Colts to the new metallic cartridges. At first he wanted to charge them five dollars each for the work, but Tom haggled until he agreed to make both conversions and give them two hundred cartridges, all for ten dollars. They would be able to pick up their pistols the following day, he promised.

"You sure won't regret switching over," he assured them as they prepared to leave his shop. I must have converted a hundred or so pistols this past year, and nobody's ever had a bad word to say about them brass cartridges. Why, I'd bet almost anything that in five years you won't see a percussion outfit anywhere!"

"You see all them newfangled Spencers in them racks?" Fergie remarked when they were once again outside. "That was them new repeaters, huh?"

"I reckon so," Tom agreed. "You load them up on a Sunday and they shoot all week long, like the little boy says. I tell you, Fergie, it was enough to turn your hair white to come up onto a nest of Unions all decked out with them repeaters. You'd think you'd run into a whole regiment the way bullets would come popping out at you, and like as not it wouldn't even be a company."

"And just think—I can remember Pa telling about when he was growing up back there in Alabama, people didn't know nothing but muzzleloaders and flintlocks!"

"That's the way it goes, boy. You don't no more than get used to doing a thing one way but what it's time to change over and start doing it some other way. Seems like everything a body learned growing up, nowadays it's either against the law or old-fashioned!"

"Maybe it would have all been different if we'd have won the war, huh?"

"It might have been, but I sort of doubt it," Tom muttered. "You mind hearing your pa talk about how it was with them cotton kings back there in Alabama, back before he went off to fight the Mexicans in '48? How they couldn't see a blessed thing but cotton, cotton, cotton? Well, that, together with the land to plant it on and the niggers to work it with. Most of them rascals, they'd have gone shares with the Devil himself to get five hundred more acres of black bottomland for cotton!"

"I remember it," Fergie agreed. "Pa, he didn't seem to put much stock in cotton or them that raised it."

Jim Harrison's return in January, 1849, from his brief tour of military service had brought to a head a conflict which had long been shaping up. His father, Fergie's grandfather, had led the family south from a rough hillside farm in eastern Tennessee twenty years earlier. The old man's death, plus the deaths of Jim's two older brothers, had left him owner of the family's two hundred acres of Alabama farmland. Lacking the time and help he needed to work the land and also fend off the attempts of neighboring cotton barons to take over the holding, he had sold out to the highest bidder upon returning to his home. He, his young brother Tom, a widowed sister and Jim's new bride—he had married just before leaving for the war—had bundled their most treasured possessions into the biggest wagon on the farm and trekked to Mobile. There they sold the wagon and mules and bought themselves a passage on the first ship to Texas.

Jim Harrison's brief tour of military service as a cavalryman operating between San Antonio and the Rio Grande had opened his eyes to the potentialities of the relatively unsettled brush country along the Nueces River. Upon landing his family in Indianola, he had sunk most of his remaining money in cattle, mustang ponies and equipment. They had delayed their departure from Indianola long enough for Ruth Harrison to give birth to young Clyde Ferguson Harrison—he had lost the Clyde long before he lost his diapers—but then moved west to a spot which appealed to all of them. Jim's sister had died in 1855, together with a husband she had acquired shortly after they had thrown up the first permanent structure on the new ranch; they had both fallen while fighting off a Comanche raid.

Fergie weighed his uncle's view of the Civil War as they again wound their way across the big plaza. None of his family had been ardent secessionists; Jim Harrison wanted only to be left alone, and Tom's decision to join a cavalry group being formed by their scattered neighbors had owed much more to youthful exuberance than to a reasoned analysis of states' rights or any of the other doctrines being argued about in 1860. Fergie had been the most outspoken secessionist in the family, but even his advocacy of that cause had owed far more to a desire to be associated with his uncle than to any devotion to political ideologies.

"You can go to it if you want," Jim had told his brother in 1861. "I seen enough of army ways in '48 to last me the rest of my life and more. Everybody ought to put in a week or two in the army, I guess, but just to see what a Godawful mess people can make out of things!"

"You know, there's something I still can't figure out," Fergie began when they had walked farther. "If it wouldn't have made no difference in the long run, I mean if we'd have won it instead of them, then what was all that fighting about? What did it all amount to?"

"I still ain't figured that one out," Tom admitted. "And you can sure bet that I put my head to it some during all that time I spent at Rock Island. What's more, I couldn't find nobody else who could tell me, either, and there was some people there who'd been off to colleges, people who read books and stuff like that. It's still a mystery to me. Anyway, it ain't nothing fit to talk about now."

Fergie refrained from giving further vent to his curiosity, though he longed to flood his uncle with more questions. He knew that the man strongly disliked talking about the recent war and his part in it; almost always he turned away direct questions with a shrug or perhaps a noncommittal reply or even a wry joke. At times, though, and especially when someone pressed him too closely, his voice could take on a very sharp edge as he turned away the questions.

They spent most of the afternoon on the plaza. There was no need for them to be anywhere else, since the corps of street vendors stood ready to supply almost anything in the way of food or drink a man might want. In addition it seemed that everyone in the city passed through the big, dusty square at some time during the day. Tom led his nephew around at a leisurely pace. They stopped from time to time in order to strike up conversations with men who looked as though they might be in the cattle business.

They learned that there were at least eight big herds, each of two to three thousand head, already taking shape for the drive to the north. The first was due to depart in about four days. They received seven offers of work with those herds, all at the rate of thirty dollars a month and board; four of the drovers offered an extra five dollars a month upon being told that Tom and his nephew could furnish three good working horses each. Tom listened carefully to each offer before explaining that their plans were not yet certain enough to enable them to make a final decision at that moment.

"Lordy, that'd be over a hundred dollars!" Fergie exclaimed after hearing the first offer extended to them. "I mean, if it really takes three whole months to get there, the way that feller said it would."

"It'll take all of three months at least," Tom assured him. "And I reckon they'll be three pretty hard months at that. You just keep on remembering what them longhorns are like, boy, and try to imagine pushing them steady for a thousand, maybe fifteen hundred miles. And don't forget to add in a few Indians, a fire or two, some gully-washing storms and maybe some outlaws. Oh, she'll be a little dandy, you can bet your bottom dollar on that!"

Fergie paid no attention to the warnings, of course. He could see only the adventure ahead; he thought little of the dust, the heat, the thirst, the hunger, the sickness and possible injury sure to be the lot of at least some of the men who were to push the cattle north. Tom did not attempt to dampen his enthusiasm further; he knew that Fergie would be up to whatever demands might be made on him.

Fergie became aware, around four o'clock, that his uncle had adopted a more purposeful walk. Fully attuned to the older man's ways, he quickly saw that his attention was directed toward a tall, buxom woman of about thirty who strolled before them. She carried a shopping basket in one hand and a parasol in the other. From time to time she stopped before a vendor on the plaza, turning just enough for

Fergie to catch glimpses of the thick pile of auburn hair, flaming red-gold in the brilliant afternoon sunlight, that framed her high-cheekboned face and a pair of deep-set blue-green eyes as striking and penetrating as any he had ever seen.

"Howdy, ma'am," Tom drawled, as he drew up beside her at one of her stops and doffed his hat. "It might be that you're needing a hand with that basket of yours there."

"Why, so I might," she said, matching his broad smile with one that hinted at mischief. "If you'd be so kind?"

Fergie watched and listened in perplexity as Tom introduced himself and his nephew. He had never seen the woman before and would have bet all his earthly possessions that Tom had never seen her before that afternoon, yet here they were introducing themselves and talking like old friends. He became aware of a strange, compelling sensation at work deep in his midsection when she looked directly at him; her eyes seemed to bore directly into his and assess his every thought. She introduced herself as Mrs. Phillips and explained that she was doing her shopping for the day.

"And it's a right lucky thing you happened to come in this direction," Tom said as he moved closer to her and took the shopping basket. "All loaded down like this, you might not ever get back home. Fergie, why don't you amble around the plaza a while longer? Keep your ears open, listen to hear what people are saying about them herds, huh? I'll see that the lady gets this basket home safe and sound. Meet you at that café right beside our hotel around suppertime, huh?"

"S-s-sure, Uncle Tom, whatever you say," Fergie stammered, aware that he had been dismissed with unmistakable finality. "I'll see you over there at suppertime."

CHAPTER THREE

Fergie watched in stunned silence as his uncle escorted the woman across the plaza. She had bought nothing from the street vendor, he had noticed, and her shopping basket contained almost nothing. He found it incredible that a grown woman could not manage so small a load, but his uncle had acted with complete assurance. He watched them stroll in front of the cathedral and turn at the corner, disappearing around its northern side. The youth frowned uncertainly as he turned back to the plaza. He bought a bottle of beer from a man pushing a cart and drank it slowly, enjoying the sharp tang of the malt.

"Suppertime" meant five-thirty or thereabouts for Fergie. He toured the perimeter of the plaza, stopping to look into almost every shop window, and investigated several of the streets leading away from the city's central business district. By five-thirty he had seen enough to make him acutely aware of the short distance his small stack of coins would take him. He hurried to the restaurant and found his uncle lounging in front of it.

"I was beginning to think maybe you'd forgot all about eating," Tom said, "but then I noticed that the sun was going down in the west same as always, so I figured nothing drastic had happened."

There was a sharp, surly edge to his voice which Fergie recognized as an excellent indicator of his uncle's bad mood. Accordingly he throttled his curiosity and said nothing, knowing that he would get little except even harsher words from the man as long as that irritable state persisted. They ate their meal in a dour silence that did nothing to lessen Fergie's appetite. Toward the end of the meal Tom's disposition brightened somewhat; the hardworking girl waiting tables helped by mentioning that the cook had a batch of peach cobblers due to come out of the oven at any moment.

After their meal they stopped at a tobacco shop, where Tom bought half a dozen black stogies. He accepted a light offered by the shopkeeper, puffed deeply and smiled again as he led Fergie from the shop.

"Ahhh, that's some kind of living," he sighed. "Another turn around the plaza to get all that food settled down good, that's what we need right now. And then let's try out the Buckhorn over there. A feller ought not to stay in San Antonio overnight without trying to buck the tiger, it seems to me. And I got me a thirst for a little snort of some good Maryland rye whiskey, too. Just for the digestion, you understand."

The Buckhorn Saloon, one of San Antonio's largest, offered a multitude of devices for separating the unwary citizen from his money. There was a roulette table, two dice tables, a chuckaluck cage and at least a dozen tables of card games. Tom turned toward the bar and inspected three bottles of rye whiskey set out for his approval, selected one and paid for it, along with a schooner of beer for his nephew.

"And a couple of glasses," he added as he accepted his change.

Fergie had more than once sampled the tequila, mescal and sotol which old Hernando Rivas distilled outside his tiny jacal on the Triple H and had a healthy respect for the power of alcohol. He found that rye whiskey, in contrast, more than lived up to his uncle's glowing praises; it was far smoother than anything old Hernando had ever created.

"Don't let that fool you none," Tom warned when Fergie had made that observation. "This stuff has got as much kick to it as any of Hernando's cactus juice but it's got manners enough not to throw you down and tromp on you right off. If we tried polishing off that bottle tonight, we'd need a wheelbarrow to get back to that hotel!"

"You know, I've been looking all day and I still ain't seen

nobody that looks like a real bad man," Fergie mused, twisting about in his chair to look around the big, crowded room.

"Huh! You reckon they'd be carrying signs around their necks? Deputies have got eyes just like you, Fergie. And anyway, you can't tell much by looks anyway. I remember one of the meanest fellers I ever saw—you'd have thought maybe he was a schoolteacher or a store clerk, just to look at him. But when it come down to shooting and fighting he was just a regular wildcat. He's about the only man I ever seen that really looked forward to hurting people, I reckon."

Fergie lifted his schooner—after sampling his uncle's prized whiskey he had decided to stick to beer—and then became aware of a man standing beside their table. He looked up and saw a man of about his uncle's age looking down at them. Slightly built and of medium height, with a very full and thick mustache even darker than his brown hair, the man had his attention focused on Tom.

"Harrison? Tom Harrison?" he asked, his voice low and soft.

"By God!" Tom exclaimed, leaning back. "Bax? Is it really you?"

"None other," the man said, extending a hand far larger than one would have expected to find on a man his size. "Of all the people I never expected to see again, you've got to be right at the top of the list!"

"Sit down, sit down," Tom urged, reaching out to pull an empty chair to their table and trying to catch a waiter's attention.

"No, don't get a glass for me," the man said, motioning the waiter away. "I haven't touched a drop in over two years. Not even beer!"

"Lordy, that's something I sure never thought I'd ever hear you say," Tom exclaimed. "Fergie, old Bax here, he used to have a gut made out of pure cast iron, it seemed like. Anything that'd run out of a bottle or a jug, he'd drink it. And drink more of it than any man in the whole damned outfit. Oh, by the way, this here's my nephew, Fergie Harrison. Fergie, shake hands with—"

"The name's Rawley, Will Rawley," the man interrupted, extending his hand and taking Fergie's with a grip that suggested ample power. "Baxter's . . . shall we say, dead? I had some, er, troubles up in Missouri last fall and thought a new name might help put them behind me. Nothing serious, you understand, but I felt that a new name and a change of scenery might be more acceptable all the way around."

"Will Rawley, eh?" Tom mused, rolling the sounds on his tongue experimentally. "All right, if you say so, then Will Rawley it'll be. Fergie, me and B—, uh, Will here, we done some fighting together in the war."

"That's putting it very mildly," Rawley agreed. "Whatever happened to you after that troop of bluebellies hit us that afternoon? Once the shooting started I didn't have a chance to see what happened to anybody except the men right beside me. Not that there was any great problem there; most of them were cut to pieces by the first volley."

Fergie sat back, watching and listening intently. Rawley—he had no difficulty in thinking of the man by his new name—lolled indolently in his chair, although there was a hint of an underlying tension in his easy manner. The youth noticed that his eyes continued roaming over the crowd around them, as though he expected at any moment to find another familiar face. Fergie also noticed the butt of a small revolver nestled under the man's left armpit as he leaned forward once; it was the first time he had ever seen a man wearing a pistol in a shoulder holster.

"It was about the same with my bunch too," Tom replied, shaking his head at the memory of that afternoon. "Everywhere I looked, it seemed like, people was dropping like leaves. I just set the spurs to my horse and set out the way we was headed. It turned out that was right toward the river. The horse took a ball in the gut before we got there but he had enough left for me to make it into the water. I just latched onto me a log and floated downstream till dark, when I hauled out onto a sandbar. Come daylight, I got ashore and skulked around some till I was pretty sure I was back in our territory and then I lit out for headquarters. After that, well, they was already breaking up our old outfit and I got put in with a troop of cavalry down south of Little Rock. I stayed with them till November of '62; that's when I got captured. Spent the rest of the war up in Rock Island, Illinois, me and about fifteen hundred more poor souls. How about you?"

"About the same, except I wasn't ever captured," Rawley replied with an indifferent shrug. After measuring Fergie for a moment, examining his fresh, open face with a pair of brown eyes as hard and expressionless as any he had ever seen, the man continued. "We stayed up in the Ozarks, mostly, raising hell with the Yanks whenever we could and trying to stay out of sight the rest of the time. What brings you two to San Antonio?"

Tom explained the circumstances surrounding their presence in the city. Rawley nodded encouragingly from time to time and offered a sympathetic phrase when he learned of the deaths of Jim Harrison and his wife. Fergie watched the man closely as his uncle spoke. Rawley represented a tangible link between his uncle and the Civil War, a topic which Fergie wanted to know much more about. Like his uncle, however, Rawley had a curious way of talking about the war as though it were something that had happened long ago to someone else. For both of them, it seemed, the war stood for something they did not want brought back to life.

Rawley spoke in a soft, almost liquid drawl with an accent Fergie had never heard before. His dark, angular face never altered its set, solemn expression, and his dark eyes registered no emotion at all. Even when he laughed, a short, barking sound which originated somewhere deep in his chest, the heavy mustache effectively covered any movement of his lips.

"So that's the way it is, eh?" Rawley murmured when Tom had finished his account. "I must have stood against that wall over there a good five minutes, trying to decide whether my eyes were playing tricks on me or not. Losing that beard and mustache, you know, you don't look like the same man at all."

"Huh? You grew whiskers in the army?" Fergie asked, gaping incredulously. "That must have been a sight to see!"

"A feller does a lot of things in the army he might not do if he stayed at home," Tom gruffly replied. "But that was a long time ago."

"That it was," Rawley agreed. "Look, if you two are foot-loose and fancy free, why don't you stop out at my camp tomorrow? There are about a dozen of us out there, some of them men who might like seeing you again, Tom."

"What? You mean to say you've got some of the old crowd together again?"

"We didn't all get shot that afternoon," Rawley told him. "Biscuit Malcom is there and Frenchy Mallet, he's along too. The three of us managed to stick together all through the war, as a matter of fact. We're about four miles outside the edge of town on the road to Castroville. Why not ride out tomorrow afternoon and have dinner with us, eh? It'll be good to see you, just for old time's sake."

He gave them more explicit directions for finding his camp, then left the table and walked out of the saloon. Tom watched him leave and then drained off the remaining whiskey in his glass.

"Well, you wanted to see a real bad man," he said to his nephew. "What'd you think about him?"

"Him?"

"Him. We must have ridden together for close to a year before we got shot up that afternoon," Tom said, pouring another measure of whiskey into his glass. "He wasn't never one to take no pleasure in killing but it sure never bothered him none neither, I can tell you that. If he'd decided to do something he'd just bull right over anybody in front of him, it wouldn't matter if it was Abe Lincoln or Jeff Davis or his own mammy. If he thought somebody was likely to be a hindrance to him, he'd put a ball between his eyes as quick as anything you ever saw. Either that or he'd slice them in two; he's right handy with a knife too, as I remember it."

"I seen his pistol hanging under his armpit," Fergie ventured. "He didn't act real friendly, somehow. It was . . . sort of like he was holding something back all the time."

"That's the man," Tom agreed. "And did you notice how that look on his face never changed none? He'd be looking exactly the same way if he was about to throw down on you. And believe me, boy, he sure wouldn't wait long to do it! If he decided that he was better off with you dead he'd do it and it wouldn't bother him no more than if he was dousing a lamp."

"That sounds a little creepy," Fergie muttered. "I mean, to just shoot somebody straight off, like you said."

"Well, there's one more difference between people like you and people like him," Tom remarked. "You might think I'm laying it on a little thick, Fergie, but I swear to God I ain't. It wouldn't bother him to kill a man, no more than it would bother you to swat a fly before it landed in your buttermilk."

Fergie found it difficult to understand and accept his uncle's assessment of Will Rawley, as the man called himself. No one had ever backed Tom Harrison down that he knew of, and he had seen him stand up to men of undeniable fierceness. Never, though, had he heard him speak of any man in the way he spoke of Rawley.

"What about . . . what'd he call them other fellers? Biscuit? And that other one? Was they all in the army with you?"

"Frenchy, Frenchy Mallet. Him and Biscuit Malcom, he said. Yep, they was in that outfit too. They weren't the peacefullest fellers on earth, not by a long shot, but for just pure hell-on-wheels mean they wasn't nowheres close to Bax, you can count on that. Come on, let's head back to the hotel. We can hit them tables some other time."

Tom grimaced and corked his bottle. He carried the bottle in his left hand as he led his nephew out of the Buckhorn. They walked back to their hotel, each wrapped in his own silence. Fergie sensed his uncle's glum mood, and knowing that it was somehow related to the appearance of Will Rawley, avoided all mention of the man. He wondered why his uncle was not more elated at having found a former companion, especially one with whom he had shared so many exciting adventures, but he knew better than to question him about the matter.

CHAPTER FOUR

Tom and Fergie had an early breakfast the next morning. Deeply imbedded ranch habits routed them from their bed by six o'clock, and they were among the first customers at the small café next to their hotel.

"Why don't you amble over to Mendoza's and see if Grayling's showed up yet with our string?" Tom suggested when they emerged from the café. "And if they're not there yet, you might take you a little ride out to see what's left of the Alamo. Or maybe head up to look at San Pedro Springs."

"All right, but what about you?"

"I think I'll listen to a couple more of them drovers and then take care of some of my own business."

"Drovers? Say, I'd like to hear what they've got to say myself," Fergie mused. "Maybe I'd better wait to see the Alamo, huh?"

"Godamighty, boy, go on!" Tom snapped, turning upon his nephew with a sudden, hot anger. "I ain't going to sign us up with no outfit yet! You just go on and leave me be, hear?"

"Y-y-yessir," Fergie muttered, ducking his head and turning away. His cheeks burned at his uncle's quick outburst.

"Fergie?" Tom called, his voice softer now. "Look, if you don't see me nowhere I'll . . . oh, I'll meet you back at this here café around noon, hear?"

Fergie jerked his head forward in an abrupt nod and strode away. He clumped across the street, heading toward the plaza, and never looked back. When he got to Mendoza's stable his own anger had subsided slightly, though he only mumbled in reply to the day hostler's cheerful greeting. He saddled Mosca, the liveliest of his ponies, and battled the spirited brown gelding to a standstill, jabbing his spurs hard into the animal's flanks and yanking up hard on the reins so that the bit dug sharply into the horse's tender mouth.

Finding the remains of the Alamo very unimpressive, he stayed there only a few minutes and then rode farther east, where he spent the morning looking over the big herds gathered on the holding grounds. He avoided the cowboys circling the masses of cattle, keeping strictly to himself, and rode back to Mendoza's shortly before noon. His uncle was standing in front of the café when he walked up; a glance showed him that the man was in much better spirits. Tom nodded approvingly when he learned that their horses were now in Mendoza's corral.

"Looks like we'll be keeping them after all," he said. "Just about every outfit I've talked to, they're a little short on good horses and most of them will pay a little extra if we've got part of a string."

"That Alamo, it sure ain't much," Fergie observed as they entered the café. "It looks like somebody's carted off most of it already."

"It never was much, at least not after the padres moved out and left it," Tom told him. "That Travis, he must have been a damned fool to have got hisself caught in a place like that, especially with all that hill country up north of here to hide in."

"That's pretty rough country up there, is it?"

"It's bad enough that there ain't no army going to go through it in a hurry. Indians, now, they can move through it pretty fast, especially a war party that ain't loaded down with women and kids and baggage. But an army, with wagons and cannons and all the gear an army carries, it'd find it a mite harder."

"Why do you reckon Travis didn't light out for the hills, then? He must have knowed that Santa Anna and all them Mexicans was around somewhere."

"Travis didn't pull out for the same reason a chicken don't hide when he sees the farmer sharpening up his ax and boiling water on a Sunday morning," Tom grunted. "Because they're both damn fools! At least, that's the way I always heard it told. I've talked to some of the old-timers, and there wasn't a one that ever thought Travis had enough sense to come in out of the rain."

"What about them drovers?" Fergie asked after devoting himself to the full, steaming plate which had been set in front of him. "You get all your business taken care of?"

"Huh? What . . . oh! Yep, I got it all settled up right nice," the older man replied, suddenly smiling with relish at the thought. "Yessirree, all settled up! Look here, boy, what do you say to us taking us a little ride out to see that camp of Bax's? Or Rawley's, whatever it is that he calls hisself now? We'll just have us a right nice little get-together with them old boys!"

"Hey, that sounds good! I was sure hoping you'd take him up on that offer of his. And maybe we could stop by too and see if our pistols are ready, huh? I'd sure like to see what kind of work that feller did."

"All right, we'll do that too," Tom agreed. "We might as well do it all up brown while we're at it, I reckon."

"Uh, last night you didn't seem to take very well to the idea of going out there," Fergie ventured as they pushed back their plates.

"No, it didn't seem like a very good idea, not right then," Tom conceded. "But what the hell, you seem to be all up in the air about it, so I reckon it won't do no harm just to go out and sit awhile."

"Say, why do you reckon Rawley's down here? Maybe try-ing to get started out with a herd or something like that?"

"Huh, if he does any cowboying it'll be with somebody else's cattle!"

"You mean, rustling?" Fergie asked, surprised at his un-cle's vehemence.

"Umm, I reckon he wouldn't go in for that, not him. To rustle cows, for one thing, you've got to know something about working cattle, which he don't, I'd be willing to bet. And then after you've made off with them, you see, you've got to herd them for a while; that's just too much like hard work for Bax to be very interested. He ain't one for plain hard work, not unless he's changed a whole lot."

"Where's he from, by the way? I don't think I ever heard anybody talk quite the way he does."

"Somewhere back in Virginia, I heard somebody say once. Not that he ever talked about it himself. I wouldn't be surprised if he'd been run out of there, wherever it was he come from. But he's an educated man, you know that? Just as polite as can be, most of the time."

"Maybe he's aiming to throw in with one of them freight outfits making up to go out west," Fergie suggested, remembering the plaza talk about the large number of merchants intending to start trading toward New Mexico.

"Same problem," Tom objected. "That's hard work too. He'd be more likely to be interested in scouting than heading up a wagon train, but there ain't no money in being a scout. No, it's a lot more likely that he's got it in mind to go down into Mexico and hire out to one side or another down there. Soldiering and hell raising, that's more his line unless he's changed an awful lot. And him having Biscuit and Frenchy along, that just makes Mexico more likely than ever. Neither one of them was ever very much on honest work either, not if half of what I heard is so."

"Didn't they make very good soldiers? I mean, that was pretty hard work, wasn't it?"

"Now right there's a funny thing. They didn't take to a lot of soldiering, the spit and the polish and the saluting and dressing up the ranks, all that kind of stuff. So far as that's concerned, you'd have to say they was pretty poor soldiers. But when it come to scouting or fighting or slipping around through the bushes, well, that was another story. They was all mighty good at that part of it."

"So, regular cowboying might be too much for them?"

"That's about it," Tom agreed. "There's people like that, boy; some of them just can't stand still to do an honest day's work, no matter what kind of work it is."

They left the café and walked to the gunsmith's shop, where they found their pistols ready. Tom paid their bill and the gunsmith then showed them how to load rounds into the chambers, assuring them that they need do no more than stuff a cartridge into each cylinder and snap the loading gate shut in order to be ready to fire.

"Most people, they only load five," the gunsmith went on. "Let the hammer rest on an empty cylinder, you know? That way, she won't let loose till you're ready. And you shuck out the empties with this rod here. Them .44s, they ought to do you fellers real well. They're the same size cartridge that goes in them new Spencer repeaters, you know, so you don't have to worry about carrying around different sizes of ammunition."

"That so?" Tom mused. "That ought to be pretty handy."

"Course these rounds ain't got the wallop of, say, one of them big .50-caliber Sharps or a Henry," the gunsmith continued, "but up to a hundred yards or so they'll put down just about anything you might run across. That's with a rifle, you understand."

"Not likely that we'll be shooting at anything any farther away than that," Tom said. "We're aiming to tie up with a herd going north. But I reckon we'd better let the Spencers wait awhile."

"This looks so easy you wonder why somebody didn't think of it a long time ago," Fergie exclaimed, slipping rounds into the chambers of his pistol and ejecting them over and over.

"That's the way it goes, son," the gunsmith told him. "Often as not it's easy to do a thing the hard way and mighty hard to do it the easy way, at least till somebody shows you how."

Fergie and his uncle shoved their pistols down into their waistbands, thanked the gunsmith and set out for Mendoza's stable. Tom put his pistol away in his bedroll, still piled in the corner they had taken for their gear, but Fergie holstered his in the big cavalry-style holster fastened to the right front skirt of his saddle. They roped out a horse each from the herd in the big corral, saddled up and led them outside.

CHAPTER FIVE

"Looks like that turnoff that Rawley mentioned," Fergie said as they approached a peculiarly twisted live-oak tree standing beside the dusty road.

"I reckon it is," Tom agreed. "About a mile north, didn't he say?"

They turned off, following a well-beaten trail, and came upon Rawley's camp in due course. The man had picked a choice location, camping on a knoll topping a gentle slope devoid of all vegetation except grass. A thick covering of brush and small live-oak trees crowned the rise. They had to ride almost completely around the knoll before they found a dim trail leading into the copse.

"This is like him," Tom muttered as he led his nephew into the thicket. "He never could stand making a camp in the open. Always had to have him a good, safe spot. Mighty hard to surprise that old boy, I guarantee you!"

"Well, I'd sure hate to try sneaking up on this place," Fergie said. "You'd have to be a real Indian to surprise anybody hid out in this thicket."

The trail led them deeper into the brush and then broadened out into a clearing that was at least fifty yards across in any direction. Someone had put up a crude *ramada* at one edge, sinking four saplings into the soft ground to make a square of uprights and joining them at the top with more poles. A thick covering of limbs stacked across the horizontal poles created a shady area underneath. Rawley lay sprawled on a blanket in the shade; he uncoiled, springing to his feet with an easy grace, as they approached.

Looking around, Fergie saw several men dotted about the clearing. Some had pistols strapped around their waists and all had new Spencer carbines in their hands or close by. Not one of them had anything like a welcoming smile on his face, he noticed; they all displayed a full awareness of his presence but without showing any interest in him as a human being.

"Get down, get down," Rawley urged. "You can tie up your horses over there. Here, I'll help you unsaddle. Stand easy, boys; didn't I tell you these fellers were friends of mine? Biscuit! Frenchy! Get over here, damn your eyes! Don't either one of you recognize an old friend?"

A pair of men stepped forward. Like their companions, they had relaxed somewhat upon hearing Rawley's reassuring words but they still kept a firm grip on their carbines. Fergie looked toward them, his attention caught by their movement, and saw a small, almost dainty man and another, much taller and thicker, advancing toward him and his uncle.

"Tom? Tom Harrison?" the smaller man asked, squinting uncertainly. "Is that really you, Tom?"

It's me, Frenchy!" Tom whooped, dropping his reins and advancing to greet the man. "Who'd you expect? U. S. Grant? And Biscuit, you old horsethief, I'd have bet money you'd be in jail somewhere by now!"

"Hell, I'd have been hung if some sheriffs was worth the money they was drawing," the bigger man replied, pumping Tom's hand with vigor. "And if you're walking around free, then I reckon Texas sheriffs ain't so hot, neither!"

"I behave myself when I'm to home," Tom chortled. "Which is a sight more than I can say for *some* people I know!"

The other men gradually relaxed when they saw the newcomers receiving so warm a greeting. A few disappeared into the bushes at the clearing's edge but most of them came toward the *ramada*, where Rawley led Tom and Fergie. They were a varied lot, the youth saw; at least two of them were Indians, wearing a combination of Indian and white garb, and there were three obvious Mexicans, as well as a couple who fell into no clear-cut category. All of them had a new repeating rifle close at hand and there were plenty of other weapons hanging over saddles scattered about.

Bottles appeared as they reclined under the *ramada*. Fergie swigged at a bottle of mescal handed him by a short, powerfully built man with a nose that had been broken and poorly set, so that there was an abrupt bend in its center. The mescal, he quickly found, was every bit as raw and violent as any liquor he had ever found along the Nueces.

"No, we don't worry much about smoothness," Rawley said, noticing the youth's grimace as he passed the bottle on. "That's another reason I gave up drinking."

"Lord, Lord, I sure never in my life expected to see all three of you together again," Tom exclaimed.

At the urging of Biscuit and Frenchy, he again described his escape from the ambush that had dealt out such destruction to their unit, then went on to mention his stay in the Union prison camp for the remainder of the war. Fergie looked more carefully at his uncle's friends as he listened once more to the tale.

Frenchy Mallet, he quickly saw, had been cut from the same pattern as Will Rawley, especially in the way his eyes and mouth reflected virtually no emotion. Biscuit lacked that quality. The man's clear blue eyes widened with interest as Tom talked. From time to time he actually laughed, his round face broadening into a genuine smile as the guffaws burst from deep inside his powerful chest. That humor might have been deceptive, Fergie decided; he remembered that it had been Biscuit who had scowled the hardest at them when they first rode into the clearing, just as it had been he who had seemed the readiest to use the rifle in his big, gnarled hands.

"Now just what in the hell is it that you're all up to?" Tom asked when he had finished his account of his experiences during the war. "All these men you got here, it looks like you're cooking up some mighty powerful medicine."

"You can bet on that," Biscuit sniggered, motioning to a scrawny, diminutive man squatting before a glowing bed of mesquite coals a few paces away from the *ramada*. "Cruz there, he's showing us a new way to cook some chickens one of the boys rounded up last night. Gutted them birds, he did, and stuffed them full of peppers and potatoes and a roasting ear before he daubed them all up with mud and popped them under those coals. Sounds like it'll be some mighty fine eating; that is, if you like a good, fat hen."

Cruz, a short, evil-looking man with only one eye—a livid red scar ran down from his left eyebrow almost to the corner of his mouth, eloquently suggesting the fate of the lost eye—grinned broadly upon hearing his name. He bobbed his head repeatedly and assured them that the chickens would be "*muy bueno*," then added a few more sticks to the coals.

"Actually, we were thinking about a trip over into Mexico," Rawley murmured.

"Mexico!" Tom exclaimed. "Hell, you ain't figuring on joining up in that war they got going down there, are you?"

"Not a bit of it," Rawley firmly stated. "I learned something in my last experience with war: soldiers are not the ones who profit from the fighting. No, I was thinking about helping out, but not quite in that way."

"We ain't soldiering no more for nobody," Frenchy added. "I done give my last salute and stood my last parade ever!"

"No more inspections for this boy," Biscuit agreed.

"I've got in mind something more like a business deal," Rawley explained. "You see, I have five hundred of these new repeating Spencers on the way up here from the coast. I managed to close an agreement last winter with a man in St. Louis who happened to be selling some equipment the Union army no longer needed. Or at least, he was in a position to certify that the army no longer needed them, which was good enough for my purposes. At any rate he sold the rifles for fifteen dollars each. To be sure, the government only saw thirteen of those dollars; the other two went to the man himself, but the government needn't know about that! I've had some conversations with an agent of Juárez who has guaranteed me fifty dollars each for those rifles."

Tom whistled his appreciation at the margin of profit in the deal but then frowned and leaned forward more earnestly.

"All right," he said, tapping the toe of his boot with a knuckle to emphasize his question, "but where's this *Juarista* agent? Where are you supposed to deliver those rifles?"

"We have agreed on a spot about halfway between Durango

and Chihuahua," Rawley told him. "I have a map showing the hacienda of a landowner favorable to the insurgents. The exchange will take place there."

"Great day, that must be six hundred miles at least!" Tom burst out. "A month it'll take you to get there, a month or six weeks!"

"Them guns won't do Juárez no good in San Antone," Biscuit pointed out. "That's where they wanted them and that's where they've got the coin."

"Well, at least there ain't much fighting between here and there," Tom mused. None that I've heard of, anyway. You might not run across any of them Frenchies, but oh my, I sure hate to think of what all else there is between here and there!"

"We expected there would be an ample supply of bandits and Indians," Rawley agreed, not at all dismayed by Tom's remark. "There will be distractions of that sort, well enough, but look: I have eleven men with me and they are all excellent fighters. We have repeating rifles and Colt revolvers of our own, Tom, and believe me, everyone here knows how to use them."

"Huh, anybody gets crossways of us, we'll start pumping out lead till they'd think they'd landed in a bullet factory!" Frenchy snorted. "Anybody who gets in our way won't live long to tell about it!"

"You'd sure better be right," Tom stated, a look of grim resignation passing over his face. "Once the word gets around what you're carrying—and it'll be pretty damned hard to make rifles look like anything else—every *bandido* in northern Mexico will be trying to fit you for a grave!"

"People have tried that before," Rawley quietly observed, "but I still sit here. Most of them are in their own graves!"

"Mmmm, you'll just about triple your money," Tom drawled after a moment of silence. "That's if you pull all this off and get out of Mexico alive. Which just might take a lot of doing, I reckon you know that already. From what I've been hearing, it's pretty much every man for hisself in that country right now."

"And that is exactly the way I would want it to be," Rawley urged. "The more anxious those other people are to look out for themselves, the less likely they'll be to unite against my project, you see. I really believe we'll be able to swing it, Tom; the chances look reasonably good. I imagine you remember me well enough to know that I don't go after something unless the chances of getting it look good enough to warrant the risk."

"I remember," Tom said, giving the man a long, deliberate look which Fergie could not fathom. "Yep, you were always one for the sure thing."

"It's the only way I care to operate," Rawley replied. "Especially when my own neck is at stake!"

"Go on, there ain't none of the others around," Biscuit urged, looking around the *ramada* and then facing Tom more directly. "Tell him about the rest of it, about Coleman and his Apache!"

"Coleman?" Tom asked, frowning. "Buffalo Coleman?"

"The same," Rawley confirmed. "It appears that Coleman went out to Santa Fe after the old outfit broke up in the spring of '65. He had spent a lot of time out there before the war, you might recall. And knowing Buffalo, I suppose you'll be able to guess that he wasn't very eager to stay in Arkansas or Missouri either after the fighting had stopped. Once he had returned to his native haunts, he—but wait, maybe I'd do better to go back to the beginning. Tell me, have you ever heard of an individual named Mustang Gray?"

"Mustang Gray, sure I have," Tom said with a nod. "A real hell-raiser from what I've heard people say about him. This was before your time, Fergie; I gather he was romping and stomping around our country a while before we got there."

"Well, I've heard a lot of the old-timers talk about him," Fergie interjected. "Old Hernando, he told me several stories about him, and I've heard some of the other hands talking about him too."

"I'd be surprised if any of them ever had anything too good to say about him," Tom grunted sourly. "From all I ever heard, he was just pure hell on Mexicans."

"Did you ever learn what happened to him?" Rawley asked.

"Mmm, I think he got hisself shot in a dustup over in Mexico. But I don't know the particulars about it."

"It was something like that," Rawley continued. "Actually, as nearly as I can find out, he got himself into a tight spot which he couldn't shoot his way out of. Here's the way I've put it all together."

Rawley launched into his story as Biscuit and Frenchy sat back, each watching to see that none of the other men came near the *ramada*. Gray, a ne'er-do-well with a penchant for violence that had made his name a synonym for terror along both sides of the Rio Grande for a time, had led a band of toughs deep into Mexico in 1844. At first content with living off the land, which they interpreted as meaning the robbery and plunder of any hacienda, *rancho* or town too weak to fight them off, they had at last wandered into the foothills of the Sierra Madres south and west of Hidalgo del Parral.

Well aware of the Sierra's rich mines, Gray and his band of toughs had ridden farther into the mountains in search of richer plunder. Eventually they had come upon a pack train carrying silver out of the fabulous *Barranca del Cobre*, or Copper Canyon, to Parral. Utilizing surprise as well as their superior firepower, Gray and his thugs had laid an ambush that resulted in their wiping out the pack train's guard and mule drivers.

"They had just finished rounding up all the mules and getting in shape to pull out," Rawley concluded, "when a band of Chiricahua Apaches jumped them. Naturally they were considerably disorganized at that moment—proving, incidentally, the value of the counterattack—and thus Gray and his companions ended up dead, every one of them."

"I've heard of them Cherry Cows," Tom remarked. "They're supposed to wander back and forth between the Sierra Madres and Arizona and New Mexico, the way I hear it. Everybody says they're hell on wheels, especially when they're fighting Mexicans."

"Ah, so it *is* credible!" Rawley breathed. "I'll have to admit that I was a trifle apprehensive about that part of Coleman's story, the part about the Chiricahuas being that far south. I'd always heard of them in connection with Arizona."

"Oh, they could be down that far easy enough," Tom assured him. "A lot of them winter down there, so I've been told. They don't seem to pay much attention to that line between Arizona and Mexico, if they ever heard of it at all. Well, old Gray dealt out enough misery in his lifetime, if half of what I've heard is so; I reckon it served him well enough, going out that way."

"What about that silver he found?" Fergie asked.

"Ah, there's a lad with an eye on the main topic!" Rawley said, fixing an approving gaze upon the youth. "The silver, yes. According to our story the Apaches dumped it in a canyon and went on about their business. Apparently they cared little for the silver."

"What does Coleman have to do with all of this?" Tom asked.

"Everything," Rawley replied. "Buffalo claims that he was trading down toward El Paso last fall and encountered an old Warm Springs Apache who was with the raid that finished Mustang Gray's career. The Indian's story is that he had some sort of trouble with his own tribe at the time and found it more, er, convenient to live with Chiricahuas for a year or two. Apparently the two tribes are rather closely related. At any rate, this Apache claims to know where this attack occurred and where the silver was dumped."

"It's beginning to make more sense than ever," Tom remarked. "You figure on selling them Spencers of yours and then you start looking for the silver, huh? What about the rest of the crew? And for that matter, where's Buffalo and that Apache of his?"

"They ought to be leaving El Paso at any day," Rawley told him. "We are to meet them at Parral on the fifteenth of May or thereabouts. As for the rest of the crew, their part is finished once we've delivered the rifles. I pay them off and we go our separate ways. Biscuit and Frenchy stay with me."

"The others, they don't know nothing about the silver?" Tom asked.

"Nothing whatever," Rawley assured him. "I believe that a few good men, very well armed, might go farther in that country than a larger force. They would be less likely to attract attention, I suspect, and they might very well be able to move faster."

"You just might be right about that," Tom conceded. "The way I see it, you'll all be rich men. I just hope you're lucky too; maybe you'll be able to spend some of that money."

"As I said, the chances appear to be reasonably good," Rawley said. "Between the proceeds from the rifles and what we can expect from the silver, the returns should be very good indeed. I'd be surprised if any of us ever had to worry for money again, as a matter of fact. Oh, there'll be rewards, Tom, very ample rewards! That's one of the main reasons I wanted you to come out here, in order to explain it all to you at leisure and let you take a look at the men I've got with me."

"Say, you ain't expecting me . . ." Tom wheezed, sitting up straighter and glaring at Rawley. "Oh, no, you can't be serious!"

"And why not?" Rawley asked, ignoring the bursts of delighted laughter from Biscuit and Frenchy, who were cackling at the look of surprise on Tom's face. "You know at least some of the country we'll be crossing and you know the language as well as something about the people. And you know how to fight, I've seen that myself. So, why shouldn't we have you along?"

Fergie, who had been following the conversation closely, almost leaped up from his seated position when he understood the full import of all that Rawley had said. The prospect of carrying a load of rifles into Mexico, perhaps fighting off Indians and bandits along the way, and then topping it off with a dash into the Sierra Madres in search of an abandoned mule train of silver struck hard at him. He could barely keep from whooping with joy when Rawley extended the invitation. Even his uncle's quick look of warning was not enough to still the enthusiastic response he felt welling up from deep in his stomach.

"I don't rightly know whether to look pleased or scared,"

Tom said after a long moment of thoughtful silence. "What strikes me right off is that we'd stand to make a lot of money real quick—and that we'd probably not ever get to spend it. Carrying rifles to Juárez, that's asking for trouble, and wandering around with a batch of silver, that's just doing it all over again. And there's Fergie too: I couldn't leave him to hisself and I for damned sure don't know that he ought to be getting into anything like what you're talking about."

Fergie's elation evaporated in a flash when he heard his uncle's reply. He wanted to yell out his willingness to take every risk, to stress his confidence that he would be able to carry his end of the load. Only the dour, warning look on his uncle's face kept him quiet. He knew that the man especially resented loudmouthed kids and he dared not risk arousing his wrath at that moment.

"It looks as though Fergie's mind is already made up," Rawley noted with a sly wink at the youth. "But that's purely a matter between the two of you. Why don't you two think it over for a few days and see if it doesn't begin sounding better, eh? And you can be thinking about this, too: I'll pay you four hundred dollars for helping out with the delivery of the rifles; you can split it up between you however you choose."

"Four hundred dollars!" Fergie breathed, awestruck by the immensity of the sum.

"As your uncle said, it might be the hardest sum of money you'll ever earn, or perhaps even the last," Rawley warned. "But, as I said, I also believe that our chances of success are good. Once we've handed over the rifles, you'll be working for shares when we go after the silver. Coleman is to get one-fifth of that, as am I. That leaves three-fifths to be divided among the rest of you, share and share alike. According to the story Coleman had from Red Shirt—that's the Apache he found, by the way—there were about forty mules in that pack train. Even allowing for Indian exaggeration, you'll have to admit that there might be a considerable quantity of silver in that canyon."

"He's sure that the Apaches just dumped it over the side

and left it there?" Tom asked. "They didn't cart it off themselves?"

"Whatever would an Indian want with silver?" Rawley asked, almost sneering at the thought. "No, they simply threw it into a gulch and rode off with the mules and their other trophies of victory. Red Shirt was quite firm when he claimed that they never saw any other Mexicans in that vicinity, so Coleman tells me. I take that to mean that the chances are good that the silver is still there, waiting for us."

"I don't know, it sounds really woolly to me," Tom muttered. "It's something to think about, that's for sure. And then too, I don't think it would be just like your average Sunday stroll, getting over to where you're going to drop them rifles off, much less thinking about the rest of it. What if them Cherry Cows is still ranging through that country? You know, the whole thing might just turn into a ring-tailed booger before you know it."

"Exactly, and that's another reason I'd like to have you along on this expedition," Rawley said. "If ever there was anyone to sit back and look a thing over very carefully, Tom, you're the man. I'm certain that we're going to need somebody with just that quality once we get across the river."

"Huh, it might not be all that easy just getting to the river," Tom retorted. "There's more than one nest of tough nuts between here and Laredo or wherever it is you're figuring to cross over. No reason why they might not start thinking about dealing in rifles themselves!"

"Ah, you see? Already you're telling me things I need to know," Rawley purred. "Excellent! Tell me, how do you stand with arms and a traveling outfit? I presume those are your own horses?"

"They're ours," Tom replied. "And we've got two more apiece in town. As for arms, we've just had our army Colts converted to shoot them new brass cartridges. Fergie's got his daddy's rifle; it's an old Spencer carbine, single shot and a .50 caliber. We've got bedrolls and a tarp, along with some cooking gear and stuff like that."

"You had the Colts converted to .44 caliber?" Rawley

asked, gesturing with approval when he saw their affirmative nods. "Good, we'll need a heavy load for our work, I shouldn't wonder. I'll give each of you a new Spencer repeater when the wagons arrive. And since you have extra horses that ought to be worth something extra, wouldn't you say? Perhaps an extra fifty dollars when we deliver the rifles? Think it over carefully and I believe you'll come around to agreeing with me all the way."

With that Rawley dismissed the subject of the Mexican expedition. His manner showed clearly enough that he wanted to hear no more about it for the moment. Fergie, on the point of exploding with excitement, dared not give voice to the thoughts and questions buzzing around in his mind; he knew that his uncle would not welcome his enthusiasm at that point and he barely managed to restrain himself. No one else seemed especially excited by the adventurous, daring plan Rawley had sketched out for them. Tom's most obvious reaction, a mild skepticism, dismayed Fergie.

"You said you'd just had your pistols converted," Rawley observed, glancing toward Fergie. "Have you had a chance to try them out?"

"No, sir, we just picked them up this norning."

"Biscuit, why don't you saddle up a horse and take the lad off somewhere so he can try his hand at shooting a man's gun?" Rawley suggested. "Do you have some ammunition?"

"Yes, sir," Fergie replied. "We was intending maybe to have a go while we were out of town today."

Tom stirred and seemed on the point of objecting, but then he relaxed and nodded his agreement to his nephew. Fergie bounded up with a leap and waited impatiently for Biscuit to untangle his thick legs and rise to his feet.

"We'll take us a little ride farther out where we won't disturb nobody," the man remarked. "We'll be back in a little while."

"Don't expect that you're going to be able to do everything with a pistol that Biscuit does," Tom warned his nephew. "He might look like a farmer but he knows something about shooting."

CHAPTER SIX

Fergie heard his uncle's warning but could make nothing of it. Biscuit looked nothing like a farmer, according to the youth's ideas of a sodbuster's appearance, but neither did he look anything like his expectations of an expert gunman. The man was dressed in simple, everyday work clothes, the sort of dress to be seen on a thousand men wandering the streets of San Antonio every day. His hat, a dusty plug which had long ago seen its best days, looked a little out of place on his square, solid head, especially when coupled with the high-topped cowman's boots of rawhide into which he had stuffed the legs of his trousers. Biscuit wore his pistol just in front of his left hip with the butt facing forward, ready for a cross-handed draw. The belt, like the rest of his costume, showed plenty of signs of age and hard wear, but the pistol had a new glint.

"You don't want to pay no attention to that uncle of yours, not when he starts to talking about me," Biscuit warned as he led Fergie over to the horses. "It always galled him, don't you see, that I was so much better looking than he was and such a better hand with the ladies and all!"

Fergie knew when his leg was being pulled and he laughed appreciatively. Biscuit certainly did not look to be a ladies' man, though he might have been a shade more attractive with a set of clean clothes—his own were covered with grease, soot and the remnants of his past three meals, it appeared—and if the wiry bristles were scraped off his cheeks and chin.

They saddled their horses, mounted and walked them out of the clearing. Once off the knoll on which Rawley had camped, Biscuit led them off to the northwest. They rode into a series of hills and quickly passed beyond all signs of settlement. Pulling up at the mouth of a small valley, Biscuit looked about with deliberation.

"Let's see that weapon of yours," he said. "Just to be sure you're started off in the right direction."

Fergie drew the heavy pistol from the saddle holster and handed it over. Biscuit twirled the cylinder and inspected the loads.

"At least you ain't got it stuffed plumb full," he grunted as he handed it back to the youth. "That there's one of the worst mistakes ever, loading a pistol up to the brim. They're pretty safe, I reckon, but you don't never know but what the hammer might just get shook a little and pop off a round while it's still hanging in the scabbard. And then where'd you be? With a hole in your leg, like as not. The idea, don't you see, is to put holes in the other feller, not yourself!"

Fergie said nothing as he accepted the heavy revolver, though he felt very happy that he had not been caught out in an elementary mistake at the very start of his lesson.

"Do you think it would be better if I had me a belt holster?" he asked after a moment. "Pa used to carry it on his saddle like this."

"That's plenty good enough," Biscuit said. "You can get it out in plenty of time if you know what's up ahead. And if you don't know, well, now, it won't matter much anyway, will it?"

"Huh?"

"Well, if they's somebody laying behind a rock down there waiting for you to ride by, then he'll stay hid till he gets a clean shot at your back and drop you neat and proper. And if he does that, then it won't matter even if you're carrying your pistol in your teeth!"

Fergie felt an involuntary shiver run over his body as he heard the man's words, uttered in so calm and matter-of-fact a way. Biscuit continued his survey of the valley and at the same time pushed five rounds out of the loops on his belt, gathering them in his left hand.

"You see that tree standing down there sort of all by itself?" he asked, pointing toward a gnarled live-oak tree on the floor of the little valley. "Now just you suppose that that was a man on foot and you was going for him. What would you do?"

"Uh, he's got a gun too?"

"Course he has, you one-eyed ninny! Least, you've got to figure he's got a pistol and a rifle and, for all you know, he's mighty good at using them!"

Fergie hesitated for a moment while he tried to dredge up an answer to the question Biscuit had put to him. The tree was close to two hundred yards away from where they stood, he guessed.

"Try a shot from here?" he finally suggested, though he was very uncertain about his answer and advanced it with the utmost hesitation.

"Not with a pistol you ain't gonna try no shot from here," Biscuit grunted, pulling a very sour face. "That uncle of yours is one of the best pistol shots I ever seen, and even he couldn't hit nothing no more'n fifty yards off. Not unless he got mighty lucky, or maybe if he was shooting at the ground."

"All right, I don't know what you ought to do," Fergie confessed. "It seems to me that if you rode up close enough to hit anything with the pistol, then he'd be likely to pick you off with the rifle a long time before you ever got there. And if you stayed back here out of rifle range, what good would that do?"

"If you stayed back you'd probably stay alive," Biscuit snapped. "And, boy, that's just what you're trying for, don't you see? All right, you've got it right there in a nutshell: the most important thing of all about gunfighting."

"What?" Fergie gaped, totally unaware that he had anything at all.

"The most important thing of all is to know when you should start popping off caps and when you ought not to," Biscuit told him. "And you'd sure better know that there's a world of difference between the one thing and the other!"

"You mean the best thing would be . . . just to turn around and leave him be? Just turn and ride off?"

"It would be the best thing if you cared anything about staying alive yourself," Biscuit assured him. "Course you could go galloping down there, yelling like a drunk cowboy and popping off rounds till you'd made a real pretty sight out of yourself, but the chances are mighty good you wouldn't ride away, not if that feller knew anything about his business."

"Would *you* ride off?"

"I sure would! Now if it happened that he was somebody I just *had* to shoot, why I reckon I'd try to get me a line on which way he was heading. Then I'd try to circle around in front of him and I'd find me a nice big rock to hunker down behind. And then, as soon as he was up close enough, I'd let him have it and he wouldn't even know I was in the same county! That way, don't you see, I'd stand the best chance of all. I could do my business neat and simple and then I'd be pretty sure of riding on to whatever else I had in mind."

Fergie nodded, though he found it difficult to accept the man's matter-of-fact recommendation of a cold-blooded murder from ambush.

"Now if it was a case of have to," Biscuit continued, "where it was him or you and there wasn't no backing out, or maybe if he didn't have no rifle, then you'd have to do it like this. But even at that it'd be a pure risk."

With that he jammed the plug hat down more firmly onto his head and drew the big Colt revolver from the holster on his belt. The regulation-size weapon looked puny in his big, knobby fist. He nudged his horse forward and then kicked the mount into a gallop. Letting out a high-pitched yell, he guided the animal down the hillside, heading straight for the tree he had earlier marked. He leaned far forward over the horse's neck as he rode and allowed the reins, clutched in his left fist, to sag loosely.

Biscuit let off three shots before getting close to the tree; Fergie saw little clouds of dust spurt up from the shots and noticed that each was no more than three or four feet from the tree. Biscuit continued driving his horse forward at a breakneck clip. He veered off to the left when he was about thirty yards from the tree, angling slightly so as to pass it at a distance of about forty feet. As he drew abreast of the tree he slipped far down onto the left side of his horse so that most of his body was sheltered behind the animal. Only his right arm, holding the pistol, and his right leg, with the heel hooked into the saddle's cantle, would have been visible to someone standing in the tree's place. When he was nearly even with the tree he peered quickly over the horse's neck and let off two shots, thumbing the big Colt so quickly that the shots sounded almost as one. He then rode on beyond the tree for perhaps fifty yards before wheeling about and again dashing toward it.

When he neared the tree again, he slipped down onto the side of his horse and fired another volley, shooting so quickly that Fergie could not count all the shots. He rode away from the tree, allowing his horse to slow down at its own rate, and then swung back up into the saddle. He lifted a big arm, still holding the pistol, and beckoned Fergie toward him.

"How'd you do that?" Fergie asked when he had ridden up beside the man. "I thought you didn't have but the one pistol?"

"I ain't got but one," Biscuit innocently replied. "Do what?"

"Do all that shooting. Does that thing hold more bullets than mine?"

"Nope, it's just a plain old six-shooter," Biscuit told him. "Didn't you see me reloading?"

"Huh? You mean you filled it up again after you shot off them first five? While you were riding away from that tree?"

"Sure I did. Boy, when the bullets start to humming and singing for real, you sure ain't gonna find anybody who'll break off just so you can get your piece stuffed full of shells again! No, you got to learn how to load her up again on the run, and how to do it in an all-fired hurry, I don't mind telling you. Now here, let's go take a look at that tree and see what kind of damage I might have done."

They rode over to inspect the tree. Fergie counted the holes himself and found six, all about chest-high to himself.

"Damn! I let off seven altogether," Biscuit muttered, looking more closely at the tree. "I was afraid one out of that second blast might have strayed off a little. Well, it ain't so bad, I reckon; if it had been a man he sure wouldn't need no more than one or two of them pills to stop his clock for good!"

"Is that what you aim for, the chest?"

"Aw, it don't matter too much, long as you're close enough. You take one of them .44 balls and put it just about anywhere in a man and it'll knock him winding six ways to Sunday. Most of the time, if you get a fairly good hit, it'll leave him in good shape to where you can stroll up easy and finish him off with a ball in the head. That's if you're of a mind to put him out of his misery, I mean."

A nervous chill ran up and down Fergie's backbone as he listened to Biscuit's easy, utterly dispassionate explanation of the effects of a .44 bullet and the various ways of making them more permanent. He could see that the man regarded killing as a thing of no very great importance. Such an attitude ran directly counter to everything he had been taught and which he still assumed to be right. His parents had not been formally religious people but they had had a very deep and permanent respect for human life. Neither of them, he felt certain, would have approved of Biscuit's cold-blooded, calculating approach to another man's death.

"I ain't saying that fighting's a good thing," Biscuit remarked, almost as though he was sensing the youth's doubts, "and I'm pretty sure that a war is pretty close to the most useless thing on earth. All I'm saying, boy, is that if you've got it to do, then it makes sense to do it so you'll have the best chance of coming out alive. Now why don't you haul out that cannon of yours and blaze away at that tree or something? It'll do you good, just to get the feel of it, don't you see."

Fergie dismounted and tugged the heavy pistol from its holster. He handled it easily enough; its weight posed no problems for him with his massive wrists and powerful forearms, which had been strengthened by wrestling with calves and horse Biscuit nodded and folded his arms, watching impassively as Fergie turned toward the tree. He lined himself up properly, extended the revolver and thumbed the hammer back to full cock. He squeezed off the shot as he had long ago been taught to do and the weapon roared. The recoil took him by surprise; the brass cartridges had much more kick than the loads to which he had been accustomed.

"Yep, they stuff a good deal of powder into them hulls," Biscuit said with a broad grin. "But I'm damned if I don't think you hit it dead center, first time off the mark!"

"Up close like this, it'd be pretty hard to miss something that big," Fergie replied, though he felt his heart warming at the compliment. "That tree can't be no more than thirty or forty feet off."

"It'd be a sight easier to miss if it was shooting back at you," Biscuit retorted. "Some people, they'll shoot at a mark and never miss. But put them up against a feller who's interested in staying alive, you might think they never even seen a gun before."

"I don't guess there's any sure way of telling beforehand which kind you are, is there?"

"Too right, there ain't!"

Fergie fired off the remaining four rounds at Biscuit's direction, scoring good hits against the tree on each shot, and turned back to his mentor.

"Now try this one," Biscuit said, nodding toward another tree about fifty yards away. "Get you five rounds out'n that box of shells of yours and, when I say so, you light out toward that tree yonder. See how you do at shucking the empties out and stuffing in new rounds on the run. Stop when you get all five of them stuck in and don't stop till then, not for nothing. Ready? Git!"

Fergie set off at a run and quickly found that Biscuit's instructions were much easier to understand than to comply with. His boots, designed for riding, made him wobble uncertainly. He managed to get an empty out of the pistol's chamber, but in trying to insert a new cartridge it slipped from his fingers and went flying off to one side. When he slowed to retrieve it Biscuit immediately bellowed out a furious oath and ordered him to keep running.

There were still two cartridges clutched in his sweating right hand when he reached the tree; he had managed to get one into the pistol and had lost another. Biscuit bellowed at him to keep running and finally he managed to get a second round loaded, though a third cartridge jumped from his fingers when he tried to ram it into the loading gate. Finally he came to a halt, some twenty yards beyond the tree, and turned to see Biscuit motioning him back.

"Now look here," the man said when they were again side by side, "suppose it was just you and me and we had us a feller pinned down behind that tree there. One of us would go after him and the other would stay back and shoot at him to make sure he kept his head down. Let's say you was going after him and you emptied your piece on the way. What in hell good would it do if you got there and peeked around that tree with your pistol empty? What'n hell you gonna do, wave it in his face and hope the breeze knocks him down? That'd get to be a shade embarrassing, not to mention being plumb dangerous!"

"All right, I can see how it might be handy to know how to load up on the run," Fergie admitted. "It'd be about the same if you was on horseback, huh?"

"You're mighty right about that. All right, let's amble on back to camp, unless you want to shoot up some more rounds."

Fergie considered the price of the rounds, then his rapidly dwindling store of money, and said that he was ready to return to camp.

"There ain't so awful much to gunfighting, most of the time," Biscuit said as they trotted their horses out of the valley. "Mostly it's just using good sense to keep from doing some damfool thing that'll get you killed. That, and being crazy enough not to know how scared you really are."

"Scared? You mean *you're* scared when you're in a battle?"

"You are if you've got any sense at all. Hell, boy, that feller on the other side, he don't have to know how to shoot good; all he's got to do is get lucky one time and you've got your ticket punched for the Pearly Gates. There was times when I wasn't just real sure about Tom or Bax, I've got to admit that, but me and just about everybody else was plenty scared when the caps started to pop. Hell, who wouldn't be scared, with bullets popping all around you and people dropping dead every place you look? Most of the people on the other side, now, they figure to be just as scared as you, so if you keep that in mind maybe you can get the edge on them and stay alive."

"I reckon a real, all-out gun battle must be pretty bad."

"It sure ain't nothing to look forward to," Biscuit grunted. "Or to look back at neither, except to be glad you come out of it alive and in one piece."

The mescal and tequila bottles were still going their rounds when they arrived at the camp. Biscuit insisted that Fergie give his pistol a thorough cleaning before joining the group; he explained that the black powder used in the metallic cartridges was every bit as corrosive as the powder used for percussion revolvers. Fergie followed the man's example and grinned with pleasure when Biscuit examined his work and pronounced it passable.

Someone had added a goat to the coals during their absence. The carcass rested on a rack made of wire, stretched over the fire, and was sputtering loudly as the heat drew grease from the meat. Cruz crouched in front of the fire, probing from time to time with the point of his knife, and daubed the carcass occasionally with a vile-looking sauce he had prepared. A pot of beans bubbled beside the goat; the two of them gave off a tantalizing aroma of goodness.

"Looks like all that stuff's getting ready for the plate," Biscuit said. "It ain't the fanciest place in town but I reckon there ain't many that eat much better. That Cruz, might be a sight to look at but he knows about cooking."

Fergie accepted half a chicken when Cruz had fished the fowl from the hiding place under the coals, plopping it and a helping of the vegetables from the hen's interior onto a battered tin plate. He added a slice of goat and a dollop of beans. Upon sampling the fare he found that Cruz's cooking was exactly as advertised: simple but very tasty. Though he had been reluctant at first to try the "mud-dauber," as Biscuit contemptuously labeled the chicken baked in mud, he found that the mud had dried into a firm crust which easily broke away from the hen, leaving only the succulent meat and vegetables.

"I ain't surprised," Biscuit snorted when he saw the look of pleasure come over Fergie's face. "When I was your age I could eat a bull's hoof and call it good!"

"I knew you wasn't very choosy," Tom pointed out. "Anybody who could eat them biscuits of yours, much less cook them, sure can't be very particular about his eating!"

Tom's sally brought a round of knowing laughter from the men, who tried topping his crack with insults of their own. Biscuit laughed as hard at the jokes as anyone, Fergie noticed.

A quarter moon had risen by the time Fergie and his uncle left the camp. The mescal and tequila bottles had continued making their rounds as the evening wore on, and Fergie felt as though there were at least a foot of open air between his rump and the saddle. Tom gave his gelding a free rein and slumped down in his saddle, his chin on his chest. Fergie tried a few remarks as soon as they had left the camp; he gave up when his tentative questions drew only a series of ill-tempered grunts. After they had turned their horses over to the night man at Mendoza's stable they walked back to their hotel. Tom glared angrily at Fergie when he again mentioned Rawley's proposal, whereupon the youth gave up and went to sleep.

CHAPTER SEVEN

"I don't want to hear nothing about that crazy idea of theirs," Tom announced as soon as he sat up in bed the next morning. "After breakfast, maybe, we'll take us a little ride and I'll tell you some more about them boys. That might cool you down a little."

Fergie had to be content with that. His uncle's eyes had a rich, livid network of red tracks, and his face had a flushed, feverish look. Tom moved very carefully, as though uncertain whether his head was really firmly attached to his neck or not. He drank heavily out of the clay *olla* on the nightstand beside their bed before starting to get dressed. Fergie recognized the signs and decided that a discreet silence offered the best course.

Tom's precarious condition did not extend to his stomach, judging from the way he attacked the steak and fried eggs he ordered for breakfast that morning. After cleaning off his plate and downing his fourth cup of steaming black coffee, he pushed his chair back and smiled for the first time in several hours.

"It's a nine days' wonder how that stuff can taste so good at night and then make you feel so much like homemade sin the next morning," he said. "You'd think a man my age would know better by this time. Come on, Fergie, let's go get us a horse and see some country."

Fergie quickly adapted to his uncle's new mood, though he still took care to avoid all mention of Rawley's proposed expedition. They walked back to the stables and saddled a horse each; Fergie noticed that his uncle selected his oldest and most trustworthy mount, a docile gray gelding.

"Let's head out toward some of them herds," Tom said as

they rode away from Mendoza's stable. "And no, I ain't going to sign us up with no outfit this morning—I just want to look them over some more and see what's what."

Two hours later, after having had coffee at one chuck wagon and exchanging words with several cowboys, Tom rode under a massive, drooping live-oak tree and dismounted. Fergie followed suit.

"Now, about that Mexico business," Tom began. "I reckon it sounded pretty good to you. Like maybe it'd be a lot of fun, huh?"

"It sure did," Fergie agreed. "I like to keeled over right there when I heard about it. And all that silver laying up there in them mountains, Lordy!"

Tom struck a match and held it to the tip of one of his stogies before answering.

"It looks to me like there's some things you maybe ain't thought much about," he said at last, expelling a thick, blue fog of acrid smoke. "Take that silver, for one. How do you really know there's any silver there at all? Some Indian says so, that's how. And it must have been twenty years ago that he was in on that dustup, that's if he really saw it at all. And even if that silver was there to start with, who's to say it's still there now? Or that that Indian still remembers how to get there? Huh?"

Fergie gulped and opened his mouth to speak, then closed it again when he could find nothing to say.

"I know Buffalo Coleman," Tom continued, "and I'd say it was just an even chance that he ever got a story like that from any Indian at all. The chances are just about as good that Buffalo's got some reason of his own for wanting to get us down there, or maybe that Indian's working some kind of dodge on his own. Or hell, maybe they're even in on something together."

"B-b-but Lordy, Uncle Tom, didn't you ride with that Coleman feller during the war? Didn't you two ride and fight together and all that?"

"We sure did and that's just exactly one reason why I'm so leery of the whole thing. Look, Fergie, I reckon it's about time you got some things straight about me and that damned war I was in. You seem to have got some notion that all that soldiering I done was some kind of picnic, or maybe a turkey shooting, where we all lined up and banged away at each other till it come time to break off for dinner and a siesta. And when we stopped to eat there was pretty girls to watch us parade and flags flying and bands playing. Well, it wasn't that way—it was a hard, dirty business and most of the time we was so wet and cold and miserable we didn't hardly know up from down, or even care much. Fact is, we was just barely soldiers at all, most of the time. There while I was up in Arkansas and Missouri, we mostly went after Union towns and settlements. You know, to clear them out so they wouldn't be around to bother us."

"I thought that was more up toward Kansas. You know, all them Jayhawkers you was talking about once."

"There was more of it up that way," Tom admitted, "but there it wasn't regular troops that was doing it; that was Quantrell and Anderson and people like that. But hell, we was doing about the same thing, mostly, except maybe not quite so much of it. And the people we raided against, they didn't have no rich friends back east, like them abolitionists up in Kansas, so there didn't nobody care too much about them and their trouble. It sure ain't a thing I'm very proud about, nor something I'd want to be told all over town. Hell, most of them people we shot up and burned out, they was just plain, ordinary folks that didn't want no more than to be left alone so they could work their crops and look after their families, that's all."

"I . . . I didn't know that's how it was," Fergie muttered, looking down at his boots. "Why them? I mean, wasn't there no Yankee soldiers around to shoot at?"

"There was bundles of them, but they was mostly to the north and east of us. The colonel, he explained about it once, said that if we raised enough hell we'd be keeping a whole mess of Union soldiers busy looking for us and guarding against us, you see? Otherwise, they could be let loose to go off into Kentucky to help old Grant and Sherman and that outfit of theirs; they was raising pure hell over that way about then."

"Lordy me, there sure is a lot to fighting a war!"

"I never had no idea how much, not till I got right smack-dab in the middle of one and by then it was too late to back out. Anyway, what I was getting around to is this: Buffalo, him and Bax and Biscuit and Frenchy, they was all part of that outfit. Hell, it never bothered them none, all that killing and burning we done; they'd as soon to shoot a farmer and burn his barn up as to do anything else. I thought it was . . . well, it *was* sort of fun at first, but after a while I just got plumb sick of the whole mess. But there wasn't no backing out, not by that time. Like as not you'd wind up getting shot by your own people if you tried to desert, and if them Union farmers was to get hold of you, well, you'd be lucky if they shot you right quick!"

Fergie twisted around to look more directly at his uncle. He saw, to his immense surprise, that his uncle was struggling hard to get the words out, as though it cost him a tremendous effort to make the admissions about his wartime duties. The realization left the youth speechless—he had never once imagined that the man might in any way be ashamed of his military career.

"Well, the long and the short of it is," Tom continued, staring steadily at the ground in front of him, "that I don't think them is the kind of people you ought to be throwed in with. Biscuit and Bax and Frenchy, they're bad enough, especially Bax, but it sure looked to me like they'd found a bunch more people just like theirselves, or maybe worse. You think about it, boy, and then you answer me this: was there a one out of that crowd that you'd want to have sit down at your mother's supper table if she was still alive?"

"Well, I reckon I see what you mean," Fergie had to agree. "There *was* some pretty scruffy characters there, but . . ."

"But what?"

"That sure did sound like it'd be a trip! Lugging them rifles all that way across there and then striking out for that silver, whooo-eee!"

"Bax always could fling the words around pretty good," Tom grunted, making a wry face. "He could start off talking about a pig lot and before long he could have you thinking it was a meadow all full of clover! Come on, Fergie, let's line out over yonder and look at a couple more of them cattle outfits. We're cowboys, not soldiers!"

They spent the remainder of the morning and half of the afternoon looking over the herds being prepared for the coming drive. By the time they headed back to San Antonio they had seen all of the herds being formed for the coming drive to the north.

Upon returning to the city, they stabled their horses and spent the rest of the afternoon lounging on the main plaza. After dinner and another stroll they took up a station at a table in a corner of the Buckhorn Saloon. Fergie was halfway through his second schooner of beer when he looked up to see Rawley slipping into a chair beside his uncle.

"Is our proposition looking any better?" he asked.

"The longer I look at it, the worse it looks," Tom said.

"I'll be around a while longer," Rawley told him, showing no flicker of emotion at Tom's short, gruff manner. "My freight is still on its way up here, so there is plenty of time remaining. I'll keep a place open for both of you."

"That's two places that'll go empty," Tom warned.

"I sincerely hope not. The chances look good but I believe they will improve greatly if I can count on you two. I'll look in tomorrow evening—maybe Mexico will look better than a herd of cattle by then."

Rawley left them alone with that suggestion. Fergie finished his beer and looked over at his uncle, expecting him to order another round. The glum, sullen look he saw on his uncle's face was enough to tell him that there would be no more beer that evening. They silently clumped back to their hotel and went to bed without exchanging another word.

Tom left his nephew on the plaza the next morning after breakfast. Fergie agreed to look in at the hotel around noon. He almost asked Tom why he needed to be alone but dared not; the memory of the man's reaction when he had pressed him too closely on a previous day was enough to choke off the question before he could frame it. Fergie spent the rest of the morning wandering about the plaza and listening to the cow talk that flowed so freely among most of the men there.

Tom appeared on the plaza shortly before noon. Fergie did not allow himself to be misled by his uncle's display of good humor when he appeared; he knew how quickly that light-hearted air could turn into a black, sullen rage. He therefore confined his remarks to the tamest, most obvious topics he could find.

They spent most of the afternoon on the plaza talking with a wide range of cowboys and stockmen. Tom asked each of them a series of questions about the drovers organizing the herds for the northern drive; he made a point of inquiring if the man had made the drive before, if he had any military experience and how long he had been working with cattle.

"It's like buying a horse by mail," he grumbled to his nephew late that afternoon as they left the plaza and walked over to the Buckhorn. "There ain't none of them fellers ever drove cattle up that far before, it seems like."

"How do we decide on which one we want to sign up with?"

"You've got to pay attention to all the other things. Has he ever drove cattle at all? What kind of wagon does he keep? What's the cook like? What do his other cowboys look like? Any man that keeps a sloppy wagon or hires him a scruffy bunch of bums from out of the saloons, he's more likely to get you into trouble than up to Missouri."

"How come you was asking all of them about whether they'd been in the army or not? You figure you maybe rode with some of them? Or against them?"

"Hell, I wouldn't mind if I never saw any of that bunch again!" Tom scoffed. "No, it ain't that. But you can reckon on maybe having some trouble with Indians or rustlers somewhere along the line. It just stands to reason that a military man, he'd be more likely to pull you out of that kind of trouble—if he was anything as a soldier, that is."

"Well, you got an idea which one we ought to sign up with?"

"I was thinking maybe that Taylor feller, the one from Goliad, he might be the likeliest trail boss. Remember him? A little gotch-eyed feller, left-handed and ugly as sin?"

"Had that little plug hat cocked down over his eye? I remember him."

"He looked like he had a pretty fair cook when we stopped out there," Tom continued. "That was the outfit that had that monstrous big wagon, the one you could haul a couple of households in. And Taylor, I heard tell he headed up an outfit that chased some Comanches halfway to Colorado back in '59 or something like that. He ought to be able to take care of his crew."

They were sitting in the Buckhorn as they discussed the various drovers. Tom had ordered a generous helping of his favorite rye whiskey, drank it quickly and called for another; Fergie nursed a mug of beer. The decision, which Fergie thought was a good one, released a certain tension within his uncle, and the man glowed expansively as he talked.

"Taylor ought to be in here tonight," he said as he finished his second glass of whiskey. "Or if he ain't in town we could ride out there tomorrow morning and get it all settled. How about us going over and chewing on a slab of steer?"

They had a leisurely meal that further mellowed Tom's happy, cheerful mood. After leaving the restaurant they joined the crowd milling across the big plaza and gradually edged their way back to the Buckhorn. They settled down at a corner table, ordered drinks and sat back to watch the crowd. Taylor was nowhere to be seen.

Fergie noticed Rawley across the big room, standing quietly against a wall and surveying the crowd; a few feet away he noticed Biscuit and another member of the crew standing against a pillar supporting the high ceiling. They ignored each other and kept their distance from Rawley, as though arrayed in some kind of military formation; neither of them paid any attention to Fergie or his uncle. After twenty minutes they still had not seen Taylor.

An hour passed and, as Tom nursed the third glass of rye he had ordered since dinner, a squat, powerfully built man planted himself beside their table. Fergie saw at once that he was no cowman; the white shirt, the carefully tied cravat and the narrow-brimmed plug hat, as well as the smooth, untanned skin of his plump cheeks and hands, marked him as a townsman.

"You Tom Harrison?" he asked in a low, gruff voice.

"I'm the one," Tom replied, looking up curiously. "Don't believe I know you, though."

"My name's Phillips."

Tom continued to look up at the man; he drew his right eye almost shut as he squinted thoughtfully.

"Pleased to meet you," he said after a moment's hesitation. "What can I do for you?"

"How about stepping outside?" Phillips suggested. "There's a little matter I want to talk to you about."

"Why, that's easy enough to do," Tom said, draining the last of his whiskey and placing the glass carefully on the table before him. "Whatever you say."

Neither of them had acknowledged Fergie's presence in any way, and they continued to ignore him. He felt an undercurrent of tension flowing between the two men, an atmosphere of open hostility, but could not have pointed to any specific word or act to pinpoint that feeling. He pushed his own chair back from the table and followed them out of the barroom, which had become even more crowded since their arrival. Phillips turned left as soon as he left the saloon; he walked to the narrow alleyway running between the Buckhorn and the building next to it, a hardware store which was closed. "Down here'll do," Phillips grunted as he turned into the narrow passage.

Two windows from the Buckhorn spilled yellow light out into the alley and gave it a semblance of illumination, though the light further intensified the already thick shadows.

"All right, Harrison, I'll make it plain for you," Phillips growled as he stopped and whirled to confront Tom. "You can get out of town tonight. If I see you again I'll take my shotgun to you."

"Huh! You think that'd cure anything?" Tom grunted, contempt plain in his voice and manner. "Hell, I ain't worrying none about it no way. If you ain't man enough to handle that Katie, you sure ain't going to cause me no trouble!"

"Why, you . . . !" Phillips grated, then threw himself at Tom. "I'll split you wide open!"

Tom stepped inside the man's roundhouse swing and planted both fists in his exposed midriff, then rattled a quick left and right off his face. Phillips staggered back, gasping for breath.

"But don't feel too bad about it," Tom continued. His voice dropped into a softer register, though it was now more clearly edged with venom. "Hell, I couldn't satisfy her neither. Why, she was after me to bring the kid along next time!"

Goaded as much by Tom's scorn as by his shaming message, Phillips again threw himself forward, mouthing incoherent cries of anger. This time he landed a blow, a looping left hand that came out of nowhere and glanced off Tom's cheek without breaking the skin. Stung by the sudden blow, Tom launched a devastating counterattack. Again he drove a series of short but vicious jabs into Phillips's midsection and then aimed a careful right hand at the man's exposed chin. Phillips went down as though he had been hit with a sledgehammer.

Fergie, who had hung back and watched the short battle with wonder, felt a movement beside himself at that moment. He blinked and then recognized Rawley darting into the alley. He bent over Phillips, examined him briefly and then sprang back to his feet.

"Tom, you'd better get out of here!" he muttered. "That man hit his head on a rock when he went down!"

"Huh?"

"He's dead! Go on, you and the boy move; I'll pull him farther back and give you a head start!"

"Dead?" Tom muttered, almost visibly swaying on his feet.

"As dead as any man can ever be!" Rawley snapped. "Go on, get your horses and gear. You can hide out at my camp tonight. Here, I'll send Corto with you; he'll guide you around town and out to camp. Where are your horses? Mendoza's? He'll meet you there in twenty minutes. Get to it now, *move!*"

Fergie felt something swell up inside his breast and then burst. Rawley's words touched off a quick reaction and he reached out to take his uncle by the arm.

"Come on," he insisted. "Let's do like he says, Uncle Tom! Come on, let's make some tracks out of here!"

CHAPTER EIGHT

Less than an hour of darkness remained when Fergie and his uncle followed Corto into the camp at the top of the hill. They unsaddled their horses, heaved the pack off the packhorse and turned all their mounts into the rude corral which had been built out of brush and ropes at the far end of the clearing. Rawley, already present, greeted them and saw that they deposited their belongings in the proper place.

"What'n hell's going on?" growled a sleepy voice that Fergie recognized as Frenchy's. "We pulling out already? Them rifles already here?"

"Rest easy," Rawley told him. "We have some new arrivals, that's all."

"Uh, what time's it getting to be?"

"Three-thirty or four," Rawley said. "Go back to sleep."

"It's bad luck for you two, getting caught like this," Rawley told them when they joined him beside the softly glowing embers of the cooking fire. "Believe me, these are not the circumstances I'd have liked for your return visit!"

"That stupid clerk, he was just the sort who'd fall down and bust his head on a rock," Tom growled. "The only thing I wonder is, why was it his head that split and not the rock?"

"He sure didn't seem to know too much about fighting," Fergie ventured. "But it was him that called the play, Uncle Tom, so why oughtn't the law to go easy on you? I mean, you wasn't no more than defending yourself, you might say."

Most of his fright had trickled away once they had horses beneath them, and by the time they pulled into Rawley's camp he had settled down enough to take a much more detached view of the matter.

"It ain't quite that simple," Tom explained. "See, that feller had some good reasons to be upset at me and so it might not work out quite that way, if it came down to a real courtroom kind of thing."

"Huh? But I was there!" Fergie objected. "I heard him call you out and, what's more, I bet there's some more people who heard it too!"

"Damn it, boy, ain't you never going to grow up? Aw, hell, Fergie, it was *his* wife I'd been, uh, sweet-talking! The law, they might say that that other feller had a perfect right to tromp me if he was able to!"

"You mean . . . ?" Fergie gasped, falling silent as the full realization slowly dawned within his mind. He remembered the tall, smiling woman in the plaza, the cool smile that had played across her lips as she had looked up at them. He also remembered and felt again the strange, tingling sensation gripping his belly as he thought of her once more. "Oh, yeah, I reckon I can see it a little better now!"

His ears reddened and burned so fiercely that he was glad the sun had not yet risen to reveal his embarrassment. He fell silent and pulled back slightly from the fire.

"The Devil's mousetrap has claimed yet another victim," Rawley said with a short, mirthless barking sound.

"Huh?" Tom grunted.

"Oh, it was only something I remember reading about once," the man explained. "It was a preacher, as you might expect, who coined the term. In his way of thinking the Devil's mousetrap was to be found between a woman's thighs."

"Oh, I get it now," Tom muttered. "Well, I've heard it called many a name, but that's sure a new one on me. Not such a bad name, though, now that I think about it! Yep, I reckon you could say I sprung that trap on myself, right enough!"

"Uncle Tom?" Fergie asked after a long silence had fallen around the dying coals in front of them.

"Yep?"

"What are we going to do now?"

"I ain't had that much time to think about it. But I reckon there ain't much future for me, at least not in Texas for a spell. It sure looks to me like maybe I'd better throw in with these boys here, at least till they get across the river a ways. You, though, I reckon you could slide through it easy enough. After all, you didn't do nothing but watch and that ain't no crime. You could probably ride back into San Antonio right now and sign on with one of them big herds and nobody'd ever raise so much as a finger to you."

"I reckon I'd rather stick with you," Fergie instantly replied. "It wouldn't be no fun, going up there without you along too. Nope, I can't say as how I'd want to do that at all!"

"Well, it sure won't be much fun following me around, keeping both eyes peeled for lawmen and not knowing when somebody's going to step up and arrest me, or maybe both of us. I think you'd better head on back into town and look up that Taylor outfit; that's the best bet for you by a long shot."

"I just ain't going to do it," Fergie stubbornly insisted, and this time he spoke more firmly, having caught a hint of uncertainty in his uncle's voice. "If you won't let me go with you, why, I reckon I'll . . . hell, I'll go back home and work for Mr. Grayling or something!"

"I don't like to intrude on family discussions," Rawley murmured softly, "but I appear to have the perfect solution for both of you. You could ride a few miles down toward Laredo, pick yourselves a spot in the brush and wait for us to pass by with our freight. Once we get strung out with our wagons, you'll be safe enough, I should imagine, and once we've crossed over into Mexico you'll be away scot-free. By the time we get across the river you'll have earned yourselves a few dollars and you'll also be certain of being out of the sheriff's jurisdiction. Or perhaps you'll have thought it over more carefully and have decided to go all the way with us; that would ensure you a very nice stake indeed, quite enough to get you a handsome start in almost any part of the country."

"Or more likely we'll end up fertilizing us a six-by-three-foot hole with our bones," Tom muttered. "That's if anybody was to take the time and trouble to bury us!"

"Nonsense! Look, I've discovered some excellent news," Rawley urged, reaching into a coat pocket and bringing out a folded section of a newspaper. "This account from Mexico City is dated less than two weeks ago. It claims that the French are pulling back everywhere, consolidating their forces around Mexico City. Doesn't that sound as though our task will be considerably easier?"

"It might do that, if that newspaperman knows what he's talking about," Tom grudgingly admitted. "Which itself is a mite risky, considering that we're putting our necks on the block because of it. All right, Bax, I reckon you've got yourself at least one new partner. Me and Fergie, we'll head out toward Laredo and hole up somewhere on the road, or just off of it. I'll figure out what to do with this stubborn nephew of mine after we get holed up. But I'll go along with you for sure, at least to the river."

"Excellent! That's the best news I've heard in quite a while!" Rawley exclaimed happily. "You can leave whenever you like—I'll have Biscuit go with you; he'll know where to find you when we leave."

"Well, I reckon Fergie and me had best be pulling out before long," Tom said. "It'll be light pretty soon, and I'd just as soon not spend too much time traveling in the daytime."

"Whatever you say," Rawley agreed. "You can help yourself to some of our supplies before you leave; you probably didn't have time to do any shopping when you left San Antonio!"

CHAPTER NINE

Rawley's men kept a pot of coffee working throughout the night and, as more and more of the sleepers came awake with the approach of dawn, another pot was added to the fire. Someone hung a pot of beans, left over from the night before, or so Fergie guessed, over the coals and flung down a sugar sack half full of cold tortillas. Each man helped himself out of the sack; some of them speared the flat cakes onto small branches and held them over the coals to heat them, while others simply ate them cold. Fergie waited as long as he could, but his hunger got the best of him before the pot of beans had heated through; he folded up a warmed tortilla and scooped out a helping of beans, then began devouring them. After finishing the first improvised taco, he helped himself to a cup of coffee and dug into the pot with another tortilla. Tom did the same, retreating from the fire to sit beside his nephew in the darkness.

They ate in silence. As soon as they had drained their cups they rose to their feet. Rawley led them over to a stack of tarpaulin-covered bundles and invited them to help themselves. They pulled out a three-day supply of food, added a couple of big canteens and carried the supplies over to their own gear. Biscuit saddled a horse for himself and waited while Tom and Fergie made their final preparations.

"We'll leave our extra horses here if that's all right with you," Tom said as he swung up into his saddle.

"They'll be looked after," Rawley promised.

With that Tom led them out of the clearing. They rode to the southwest, with Biscuit and Tom watching for riders, and kept up a steady pace for three hours. They rode into a rolling country, full of draws and thickly clotted with brush and trees, and stopped on a slope about half a mile from the Laredo road. A small creek, clear and fast moving, ran at the foot of the slope, assuring them of an adequate supply of water.

"All right, I'll come looking for you when we're ready to pull out," Biscuit said as he prepared to leave. "Bax, he reckons them rifles ought to be here just about any time, so you boys stay close to home, hear?"

"We'll do it," Tom agreed. "You won't miss us when you leave, not by a long shot."

Biscuit waved and trotted his horse off in a southerly direction, never once looking back at them. Tom unsaddled, then motioned for Fergie to help him unload the packhorse.

"Don't break the pack open," he muttered as they loosened the hitches. "In a couple or three hours we'll be moving on again."

"Huh? B-b-but how'll Biscuit and them find us when they get ready to move?"

"They won't. We'll find them."

"Hey, there's something going on around here!" Fergie exclaimed, grunting as he helped ease the heavy pack to the ground. "And I don't understand none of it!"

"If there's going to be lawmen looking for me, then I'll feel a sight safer if I'm someplace that *nobody* knows about," Tom replied. "It'd take a good two or three hours for one of Bax's men to get into town and for a deputy to get back out here, so we'll just sit tight here for a while and take it easy. And then we'll move to another spot and we'll start watching. We'll watch the road for Bax's outfit but we'll watch this spot here too, just in case."

"Say, you really don't trust them fellers much, do you?"

"Well, you don't know but what that feller in town, that Phillips, he just might have had him enough friends for them to have got together and raised a little bounty for my pelt," Tom pointed out. "It ain't likely, I admit that, but it's a chance I don't have to take. Hell, I wouldn't be a bit surprised if most every man in that bunch back there ain't collected him a bounty or two at some time or another. And

I know something else, too: if they was all honest, upright citizens they wouldn't be throwed in with Bax!"

"I reckon maybe if a deputy don't show up around here, then that ought to go some to showing that Rawley's really playing square with us, huh?"

"Now you're starting to figure things about right!" Tom told him. "See, it ain't so hard to think just like a crook, not if you put your mind to it a little and try!"

Fergie grinned with pleasure at the remark, which he took to be a grudging sort of compliment, and began looking for a suitable spot from which to watch for intruders. His uncle directed him to a spot across the creek, far up the slope on the opposite side, and pointed out the spot he had chosen for himself.

"Once you get there you just sit tight and watch," Tom ordered. "Leave your gun here; we for damned sure don't want no shooting. And keep still too—there ain't nothing to give you away quicker than hopping around like a bullfrog on a hot stove lid. Whistle if you see anything, but make mighty sure you know what you saw. Clear? All right, now get to it!"

Fergie scrambled across the ankle-deep stream and made his way up the slope, looking back from time to time to make sure that he was still going in the right direction. He found a spot under a low-sweeping oak tree and settled down, first making sure that he was not placing himself in an ant bed.

Two hours later—it seemed like half a day but he could tell from the sun that no great amount of time had passed —he heard a whistle and looked over to see his uncle waving him in. He left his post and again crossed the creek.

"I didn't see a blamed thing but a couple of white-tailed deer and a milk cow," he reported. "It sure looks like people done forgot all about this end of the world."

"I didn't see nobody neither and I ain't complaining a bit," Tom replied, picking up his saddle and moving toward his horse. "We'd better get us a move on—somebody'll be out looking for that milk cow, most likely, and the less people I see the more it suits me from now on."

They saddled up, loaded the packhorse and mounted. Tom led his nephew upstream, cautioning him to watch carefully. "Just look for anything that don't fit," he said when Fergie asked what he should be looking for. "We'll figure out what it means after you see it."

Fergie looked until he felt sure his eyes were going to pop out of their sockets but he could find nothing unusual in the scenery passing before his eyes. Mockingbirds flitted through the brush, singing loudly; squirrels barked angrily at their intrusion and scampered about on nearby limbs, switching their tails with nervous energy. Tom walked his horse up the stream's bed, motioning for Fergie to do the same, and they stayed in the water for at least half a mile. Tom presently bore off to the west and moved into another little valley, one that ran in almost a due north-south direction. After another hour of slow traveling he turned up a slope and rode almost to its crest. He kept to the trees and brush as far as he could and, before crossing an open space, he took plenty of time to scour the landscape in every direction. Finally he rode down the other side of the hill and stopped at a small clearing.

"This looks like as good a place as any," he said as he dismounted. "We'll be as safe here as anywhere, I reckon."

"There's about one little valley and a couple of ridges between us and where we was before, ain't that so?"

"You called it. I didn't figure it would be very smart for us to move just one valley over; they might want to circle around and come at us from the blind side and there we'd be, all spread out and waiting to be caught. This ought to give us a little more breathing room."

They stacked their saddles, bridles and pack under a tree and staked their horses at one end of the clearing. Tom cocked an eye at the sun and then dug into one of the sacks they had taken from Rawley's pile of supplies. He handed out a couple of cold tortillas and poured a portion of pinole into his nephew's outstretched palm, then took a similar helping for himself. They washed the food down with swigs from their canteen and called it a meal, once they had sliced off a strip of jerky to gnaw on during the afternoon.

"Better save that pemmican for supper," Tom said. "Eat too much of that stuff now, and you'll likely go to sleep watching this afternoon."

"We going to keep guard again?" Fergie asked, dismayed at the thought of spending the entire afternoon nearly motionless.

"You're mighty right we are," Tom said, frowning, "and we'll be doing a lot more of it for a long time to come, at least until we get to where we can be pretty sure there won't be no deputies around. You're getting you a taste of soldiering, boy; don't you like it none?"

"Well, it gets a little tiresome, just sitting still there and looking," Fergie admitted.

"It'd get a sight more tiresome just laying in a grave and listening to the grass grow," Tom snorted. "And that's what happens to soldiers who don't keep a good watch, them and outlaws too, I reckon. First thing you know, here'd come a bunch from the other side and wham! they're peppering your gizzard with lead. The best way to keep that from happening is to keep both eyes open all the time."

He pointed out the general area in which he wanted Fergie to locate his guard post, one that would allow him to spot the dust of anything moving on the Laredo road, and he indicated the spot he had selected for himself. They went their separate ways and did not see each other again until dusk was settling over the valley.

"It gets a little dull, don't it?" Tom asked when they met again and sat down for their cold supper. "Just sitting there and trying to keep still, that gets old in a hurry, huh?"

"Toward the end there I was sort of hoping maybe somebody'd come along and liven things up, just so's it'd be a little different," Fergie acknowledged.

"Time you've lived through an attack or two you might be hoping there wouldn't nobody *ever* come along! Hell, we was lucky—this was a nice day. You just put your mind to thinking about how it'd be if it was raining, say, and there was a good, stiff breeze whipping down out of the north to where you could tell there was snow up thataway. Say, if your feet was wet and you felt like you wouldn't never be warm again and you knew damned well that your bedroll was wet too and there wouldn't be no fire that night to warm up your supper or to toast your feet by—that'll give you an idea of what it *can* be like. Yeah, and don't forget to add in some Yanks or Indians or somebody else crawling around out there in the dark, just hoping you'll go to sleep long enough so they can get up close to you and slit your throat!"

"Lordy me, Uncle Tom, you make it sound like the worst thing on earth!"

"Somebody told me once that old Billy Sherman said that war was hell, and I can tell you, Fergie boy, he knew just exactly what he was talking about. War *is* hell, it purely is and there ain't no two ways about it. Here, let's break into that pemmican and see what kind of cook it was that Cruz found for us."

Her pemmican was exactly as advertised, they discovered. She had made it the Indian way, even down to using rawhide boxes. She had poured an inch of melted buffalo tallow into the bottom of the oblong box, then added a layer of finely flaked jerky, another of shelled pecans and berries, another of tallow and so on, alternating the layers until the box was full. The melted tallow had run down through the layers of nuts, berries and meat, holding the mixture together and giving it a firm texture.

The pinole, cornmeal mixed with brown sugar, bits of dried fruit and pieces of nuts, complemented the pemmican perfectly. They ate the last of the leftover tortillas and again washed the mixture down with cold water from their canteens.

"Whooo-boy, that woman sure knows how it's done," Tom said as he cut off another cube of pemmican for them. "We'd be fat as bears in the fall if we had stuff like this every day!"

"It's pretty good eating," Fergie agreed. "Uh, we going to stand guard again tonight, Uncle Tom?"

"No, I reckon we'll just have to take our chances after

dark. They look fairly good, by the way. Them deputies ain't likely to try no night work, so we ought to be able to rest pretty easy tonight. But it'll be more of the same tomorrow, so don't fret yourself about that."

They finished their meal quickly, led their horses down to water and then staked them out on a new section of turf. It was fully dark by the time they had finished those chores, and they had to shake out their bedrolls by feel. Fergie lay on his back for a few minutes, watching the pattern of wind-chased clouds play against the quarter moon, and gradually slid into unconsciousness.

"A little cup of coffee would go right nice this morning," Tom muttered as he pulled on his pants and stamped about in the chilly half-light of the next morning. "And a big one would go even better. It's a damned good thing Bax didn't give us no coffee, I reckon, or else I'd surely be tempted to brew us up a little batch."

"A fire wouldn't be very smart, I reckon."

"The only worse thing would be to start shooting off our guns and yelling for company to come. If anybody happened to be looking for us, they'd surely keep an eye open for a fire at this time of day."

Fergie spent a great deal of time in thinking about his future while maintaining his surveillance of the country around them. He longed to press his uncle on the subject, to inquire into his thinking, but dared not; the best strategy, he knew, would be to avoid all mention of the Mexican venture and wait. Several times it seemed that Tom was about to bring up that topic, but each time he clamped his lips together and lapsed into a lame silence, leaving Fergie almost beside himself with anxiety.

At nightfall of their third day in the brush, after they had eaten all but a handful of the pinole and a small portion of the pemmican, Tom gauged the remaining supplies and muttered something under his breath. He stood up and walked away from their bedrolls; Fergie knew the outward signs of an inner turmoil and stayed firmly seated on his haunches.

"I'll head over to their camp tomorrow morning and get us

some more supplies," he said when he returned to their bed-rolls. "It looks like we're running a mite short."

"I could go," Fergie offered. "I mean, them deputies wouldn't be so likely to be looking for me, would they?"

"No, I'll do it," Tom insisted. "I'd go tonight except I ain't sure I could get out of this rat's nest of hills and draws at night without riding into somebody's front yard. You go on to bed and don't worry none about it."

He had not been out of sight more than two hours the next morning when Fergie heard his whistle from their campsite. Hurrying down, he learned that his uncle had ridden by their first campsite and had found Biscuit waiting there.

"He'd brought us another sack of grub," Tom said, untying the thong which held a well-filled sugar sack to his saddle-horn. "And somebody's finally got word about them rifles—they ought to be here today or tomorrow for sure, so we'll be pulling out before too very long."

Fergie thought his heart was going to pop up into his throat when he heard that. At once he wanted to cry out, "What about me?" and almost did so, though he managed to choke off the question just in time.

"I bet they was starting to wonder if maybe somebody else was going to go into the rifle business on their own," he managed to say instead.

"Huh, anybody who tries that on old Bax, he'll get out of it a hell of a lot quicker than he went into it," Tom said, grinning wickedly at the thought. "And he won't never be getting into no other business, either! Except feeding worms, maybe, and that don't pay worth a damn!"

"Uh, they still don't want us to help unload and reload that stuff?"

"All right, I know just exactly what you're driving at, you lop-eared pup! Here, we might as well have us a sit while we talk all this over. It seems like there's some parts to all of this mess that I hadn't heard about before. They make a differ-ence, too."

Fergie plopped himself beneath a tree and waited, knowing that he would hear all of it in due course and, surprisingly, displayed good patience. Tom sprawled beside him and began, grimacing from time to time as he talked. He said that Rawley had gone back into San Antonio the day after the fight with Phillips and had learned that deputies were looking for a *pair* of killers.

"And you can just guess who that pair mostly looked like," he added.

"I reckon there was enough people around who knowed we was together," Fergie said. "So now they figure we both done him in, huh?"

"It looks like that's the way it is. Anyhow I'm just damned glad now that you didn't go back into town and try hitching up with Taylor's herd. And it looks like the home place wouldn't be a very good spot for you to be at, neither—they'd likely start looking down thataway once they didn't find us with any of them herds."

"Uh, what do you reckon I ought to do?" Fergie asked, holding his breath with anticipation.

"Hell, there ain't nothing else to do. I reckon you'll have to throw in with us and try to get across the river, boy."

"Whooo-eee! Hot damn, that's the way to talk!"

"Huh! You might wind up thinking a lot different before you get there! Well, that looks like the best ticket, anyhow. Fergie, I'm just as sorry as anything that this all had to happen. I surely don't know how I could ever look anybody in the eye and admit that I was standing in for your mammy and daddy, what with the mess I made out of things, but I just don't see how there's anything else for us to do."

"By damn, there ain't nothing else on earth I'd rather do!" Fergie exclaimed, rocking back and forth on his rump and clutching his knees. "I tell you, Uncle Tom, you sure won't have to worry none about me. I'll keep my eyes open like nobody's business and . . . hell, I'll even harness up mules and drive a wagon! Yessirree, I'll show you just how right you really are!"

CHAPTER TEN

If Fergie found a new and wild elation in his uncle's decision, Tom showed an opposite reaction once he had made his choice known. For the rest of the day he had a sour, glum expression, and he had little to say when they met at dusk after having spent the day watching the surrounding hillsides and valleys. Fergie's high spirits survived even a sharp retort and an order to "shut your yap!" when he pushed his uncle too far. They went to bed as soon as they had fed themselves and watered their horses.

They went out the next morning to stand their hours of guard duty and saw no sign of anyone searching for them, nor did they mark any significant amount of dust moving to the west along the Laredo road. The next morning, however, Fergie noticed several plumes of dust very early; they were all moving in a westerly direction. He went to get his uncle and they decided to pack and ride down to make sure the dust had been raised by wagons.

"No need to hurry all that much," Tom said as they set out at a walk. "You don't figure on them wagons making very good time."

"We ought to catch up with them in a couple or three hours, huh?"

"Maybe. We'll take our time, though, and ease around to come up on them from behind. It won't hurt to check out the back trail."

They trailed the wagons, keeping a mile or two behind them, for most of that day. Finally, when Tom was satisfied that no one was following, they spurred ahead and came upon the wagons as the sun was falling behind the horizon.

"You just amble along at a walk with the packhorse," Tom

told his nephew. "I'll drop back and get on a hill somewhere so I can watch the back trail. And don't worry none about it; I told Biscuit about it the other day when he brung us that sack of grub. They know what we're doing."

Fergie consoled himself as best he could while he herded the loose horses along the road. They camped that night in a thick patch of mesquite, well away from any semblance of a trail; of course they did without a fire and they slept soundly.

"We'll camp with the rest of the boys tonight," Tom said as they divided most of the remaining food the next morning. "If I ain't seen nothing by then, we ought to be in pretty good shape. Don't hurry to catch up with them, though; if there's somebody following, you sure don't want to get caught with none of that bunch."

"But mightn't they need us there? You know, to help out with the horses and stand guard and all like that?"

"We're doing them boys plenty of good right where we are. And hell, if they was to run into trouble we'd do best to stay out of it altogether."

"But we done said we'd throw in with them!" Fergie protested, outraged at the disloyalty implicit in his uncle's remark. "Why, they'd come help us if we got into trouble, wouldn't they?"

"It'd all depend on how much they figured they needed us and how much it would take to get us out," Tom said, openly amused by his nephew's bold attitude. "Look, boy, it's just a straight business deal, and if the odds start to looking too bad we'd do best to cut our losses and slide on out. That's just exactly the way they'd deal with us and it had better be the way we deal with them. So don't go figuring you owe Bax and the rest of them boys your last penny."

Fergie turned away to gather the horses but he did so with a show of temper which plainly indicated his disgust with his uncle's recommendation. He could not conceive of Biscuit, for example, who gave every indication of being as straightforward and dependable as anyone he had ever seen, deserting either of them if they happened to be caught in a tight spot. He promised himself that, as long as he had anything to say about it, he would not desert a single one of his new comrades, no matter what the occasion or the odds.

The day passed slowly. Fergie did not see his uncle again until late that afternoon, when he rode up from the rear. His horse was sweating heavily and blowing.

"I sat back there a ways to see if anybody was five or ten miles back," he explained. "Time nearly got away with me and I had to hump it a little to get here on time. Let's go find them wagons."

They came upon the wagons as the sun was falling behind the horizon. Rawley had pulled off into another of the small valleys which were so numerous in that area; the cooking fires were going when Fergie and Tom rode up, though they were heating nothing more substantial than coffee. They unloaded their packhorse beside the wagons, walked the mounts over to the remuda and then joined the men around the campfire.

"Good to see you," Rawley said, nodding to the coffeepot bubbling on the fire and pointing to a stack of tin cups. "Help yourselves."

"There wasn't nobody following," Tom told him. "Or if they are, they're sure keeping their distance good. I ain't seen nobody but a couple of cowboys and Fergie for the last two or three days."

"I reckon that must be why you're so down in the mouth," Biscuit said, directing a sly wink at Fergie as he spoke.

"Yep, that's enough to get anybody soured on the world," Frenchy added, cackling with delight.

Fergie grinned, recognizing that their banter indicated a measure of acceptance. He said nothing, basking in the attention thus given him.

"We're mounting two-man guard posts," Rawley told them. "One down by the horses and the other in the woods behind us; both men to watch the meadow in front of us. They are two-hour shifts."

"Just like the old days," Tom commented. "All right, when do we start?"

"I suggest a drawing as soon as we finish eating," Rawley

answered. "Now that we're at full strength we ought to get ourselves settled down into a routine."

"What kind of lookouts do you keep while you're moving?" Tom asked.

"Two men on each wing, about a quarter of a mile to either side of the road; a man ahead, a quarter of a mile but on the road; the rest of the men on the wagons or behind them. I don't mind saying that you . . . well, there will be plenty for you to do, don't worry about that!"

"Sounds good to me," Tom said. "You're calling the shots."

Except for a quantity of hot coffee, their evening meal offered exactly the same menu Fergie and Tom had had ever since pulling out of Rawley's original camp: jerky, pinole and a square of pemmican per man. The latter was so rich, so heavily laden with nuts, berries and the tasty buffalo tallow, that it was almost a confection; the strong black coffee made it better than ever and also made the pinole considerably more palatable.

Rawley held the drawing for guard slots as soon as they had finished eating. He scribbled numbers onto tiny scraps of paper, dumped them into a hat and held it out for each man to draw his post. Fergie found that he had drawn a one; he decided to wait until the drawing was over before asking what it meant.

"You get the first shot at it," Rawley told him when he showed him the number. "That ought to be, oh, from about seven o'clock until nine. You must have been living right to have drawn so excellent a slot."

Fergie found that his partner for guard duty was Frenchy. There was very little time before they were to begin their tour of guard duty; Fergie spent it in conferring with his uncle about what he should do.

"Just move around a little and keep your eyes open," he was told. "For God's sakes, don't start shooting, no matter what. And don't let Rawley catch you snoozing—he's liable to try sneaking up on you just to make sure that you're really on your toes. He can move like a cat, I'm telling you. Just use your head and don't try to be a hero, that's about all there is to it."

"Uh, what's so good about drawing this turn?" Fergie asked. "I couldn't make out why he said that."

"Figure it out," Tom replied. "This way, you don't have to get up in the middle of the night. And most likely you wouldn't go to sleep much before you get off your turn anyway, so it's almost like you wasn't standing guard at all."

Fergie pulled his pistol out of the saddle holster and stuffed it into the front of his trousers, after checking it to be sure that the hammer still rested on an empty chamber. Rawley assigned him the area in the woods near the wagons, going with him to mark out the approximate area he was to patrol; Frenchy was told to stand guard down by the horses. Fergie used the few remaining moments of dusk to explore his appointed area. He found that he could make himself a circuit that covered a stretch some thirty yards wide and two to ten yards deep into the undergrowth. He practiced moving as quietly as he could and varied his pace, sometimes remaining in a deep shadow for several minutes and then continuing on to the edge of the area he had marked out for himself. At the end of the second hour Rawley whistled them in; Fergie had seen nothing suspicious.

They soon settled into a daily routine, just as Rawley had hoped. Tom was assigned to one of the outrider posts and spent his daylight hours well away from the wagons. Rawley had set up a rotating pattern for the guards, so that no one rode for more than three hours in the same spot; he told Fergie that this was to ensure that the guards would stay alert. Fergie drew an assignment to help with the horse herd.

"Tom said that you were a pretty good hand with horses and Paco needs some help back there," Rawley told him. "He'll show you what to do. The main thing is to keep them out of the wagons' way and to let them graze as much as they can during the day. Of course you'll also keep watch for anything the guards might miss but your main concern is the horses and mules. They might become extremely valuable to us later on; we need to take good care of them."

Paco, a bony, string-thin man who could have been anywhere from forty to sixty years old—his hair, rank and as
straight as an Indian's, was jet-black, but his face was a network of wrinkles and had a dried, leathery look, like a boot
which had been left out in the sun too long—shrugged indif-
ferently when Fergie told him of his assignment and motioned him to take one side of the remuda. At noon they
brought the herd up to the wagons, where each teamster
selected a fresh pair of mules and turned the morning's team
in with the rest. They had enough mules, Fergie calculated,
that no mule would have to work more than half of every
other day.

"Sí. We eat them bitches before long," Paco grunted when
the youth mentioned the large number of mules in the remuda. "Too many now; we work them good and then,
mmmm!"

He licked his thin, lizardlike lips in anticipation of what he
evidently considered a feast. Fergie, who had never tasted
either horse or mule meat and had no desire to do so, shivered
and turned away. That night, as he sat beside his uncle while
eating supper, he mentioned Paco's plans for the beasts.

"He must be about nine-tenths Indian," Tom said, smiling
at his nephew's disdain for horse and mule meat. "There's a
lot of Indians that relish a nice dish of horse or mule, the way
I hear it. Apaches, they tell me, they'd rather have a helping
of mule than most anything. And you know something?
They won't eat a fish for nothing!"

"Mmmm, wouldn't a big old platter of catfish and corn
dodgers go down good?" Fergie muttered, gazing into the
darkness. "Maybe with some molasses to sop them dodgers
in and a big, red onion, whooo-eee!"

"I reckon you can say good-bye to a catfish for a good long
time," Tom advised. "The rate we're going, I doubt if we'll
have any time to do any fishing, and once we get across the
Rio Grande I'd be mighty surprised if there'll even be enough
water to grow pollywogs!"

Rawley kept them at a hard pace. He wanted to cover the
distance between San Antonio and the Rio Grande, about

150 miles, in a week, and he had them moving each day by the time the sun had cleared the eastern rim of the hills behind them. During the day they stopped at noon, but only long enough to change teams, and they kept going until almost dark.

Fergie estimated that they were averaging almost twenty-five miles a day, a guess which Tom confirmed. On the fifth day out of San Antonio they forded the Nueces, the only sizable stream before Mexico unless the Frio happened to be running strong; Fergie felt a momentary touch of sadness when he thought of following the river downstream until he came to the Triple H and all its familiar scenes. Paco effectively diverted his attention by whistling sharply and pointing to a dappled gray mare which was edging away from the main herd; he spurred his own horse after her and quickly forgot about home.

Tom had already conferred with Rawley about their route, and as soon as they had the wagons across the Nueces they bore right, taking a due west course that would have them approaching the Rio Grande at a point about halfway between Laredo and Eagle Pass. One man rode ahead, searching for the easiest path for the wagons, and the others stayed closer to help when needed. They left the road behind them and began cutting across country, and several times the riders had to hitch their ropes onto the wagons to help the mules negotiate a rough stretch. Their mileage dropped accordingly and Rawley became more on edge with every hour.

"Two more days, maybe," Tom said when Rawley asked about the distance to the Rio Grande after leaving the main road. "But if we run across any more stretches like that last one this afternoon it might be a week!"

They had spent a sweaty, sweltering hour in pulling the wagons through a wash, getting everyone in a bad mood, and had then plunged directly into a long stretch of sand which had extended for miles, or so it had seemed.

"The extra time will be worth it," Rawley said, though he plainly regretted the necessary delays. "I wouldn't have wanted to put us much closer to a town. The more people there are the more questions there will be—and we do not need people asking questions about us or our cargo!"

He cautioned the guards the next morning to be extra diligent from there on and he reminded them about the likelihood of patrols from the army posts at Laredo and Eagle Pass. They saw no trace of any military activity, except for some sign which was at least three or four days old and not definitely army, and made good time even without the convenience of a road. They arrived at the Rio Grande at almost exactly high noon on their eighth day out from San Antonio.

"Keep those wagons well back in the brush here," Rawley ordered when he rode up onto the crest of a hill and spotted the river ahead, stretching out in pools like a glass beaded necklace. "Frenchy, ride back and tell Paco to hold the horses back there. Tom, you and Biscuit see what the footing is like and then investigate the other side."

He sent other men upstream and downstream, ordering them to find good lookout posts at least a half mile away and to begin watching carefully for army patrols and any other intruders.

"Watch yourself and keep a rope handy while I look it over," Tom said to Biscuit as they trotted their horses down to the river.

"Hell, it don't look like nothing much," Biscuit said, eying the broad but shallow expanse of dark brown water.

"Don't let it fool you none," Tom warned. "Some of them puddles can get pretty deep and there's patches of quicksand that don't have no bottom at all!"

They found that the river was nowhere more than knee-deep on their horses; in most spots it was less than half that. The water ran in three main channels at the spot they began investigating; upstream and down it bellied out into occasional broad pools and then regrouped into another pattern of channels. They rode back and forth for a quarter of a mile, searching for a stretch of rock and gravel that would give a firm footing for the wagons, but had no luck.

"Looks like we just might have to double up on them mules," Tom said when they decided to give up the search.

"They'll just have to hump them wagons across the best way they can in the mud. Come on, let's see if there's anybody waiting to meet us on the other side."

They searched an area a mile deep and extending half a mile on each side of their crossing and found no trace of human life. Biscuit reported finding a tumbledown jacal, made of mesquite branches woven around uprights, but said it did not look as though it had been inhabited for several months.

"Odd thing, finding a shed like that without no house around," he mused after giving his report to Tom.

"Hell, that *was* the house, most likely," Tom snorted. "People over here, they ain't got so much money to spend on houses and such. They live in places a self-respecting Missouri farmer wouldn't even keep his chickens in!"

"Well, if people lived there they sure must have loved the out-of-doors," Biscuit retorted. "Because that's just about what it was!"

They recrossed the river and reported their findings to Rawley. He gave his orders as soon as he heard what they had to say.

"We'll double up on the teams," he said. "Biscuit, tell the teamsters to start rehitching. Frenchy, go find Paco; tell him to get the herd up here and to hold them near the crossing. As soon as we get a wagon out of the river, pull it up out of sight. Then unhitch and bring the harness back; we'll use fresh teams once the old ones are across. Tom, gather up everybody who's not doing anything else and get them over there. Spread them out and mount a guard; we do not want any surprises while we're crossing the wagons."

"You might ought to keep a couple of men with good, stout horses in the river," Tom suggested. "Just to help out in case a wagon gets bogged down, you know. That bottom ain't nothing much but pure mud and sand, so it's going to be a booger for the last wagon or two."

"Very well, you pick them out and tell them what to do," Rawley agreed. "Now let's get to work and get ourselves into Mexico."

The crossing went off almost as smoothly as Rawley had outlined it. One wagon seemed mired for a moment, but the teamster unlimbered his big whip and used it artistically; the wagon was moving again before the nearby riders could get their ropes onto the wagon. Within two hours from the time they had sighted the Rio Grande they were all inside Mexico and on their way again. They made camp that night on a barren patch of sand several miles away from the river.

CHAPTER ELEVEN

Fergie saw a different side of Rawley on their first morning inside Mexico. The leader had been pacing back and forth near the fire as the men ate their breakfast, drank their coffee and rolled their blankets for storage in the wagons during the day. He followed a group over to the horses and watched them rope out their mounts.

"Medlow, that saddle blanket is a disgrace," he snapped to a tall, thick-shouldered man who was reaching down to pick up his gear. "Get another one. Use one of your own blankets if you must."

"Aw, go to hell, this one'll do for another month or two," the man retorted, looking up angrily. "And besides, my horses ain't done no complaining about the shape this blanket's in!"

"Look at the back of that animal you've roped out," Rawley told him, his voice becoming softer. "There will be a saddle sore there by nightfall."

"Just shut the hell up, will you? Hell, there's plenty of horses in this string, enough for everybody to waste one or two. And anyway, I had me about enough of your infernal bellyaching! You just go on and mind your own damned bus—whupp!"

Fergie saw only a blur as Rawley uncoiled like a striking rattler; he had a vague impression of a fist thudding into Medlow's prominent jaw, sending the man staggering back on his heels. Medlow grunted out an angry oath and reached for the pistol hanging at his right hip. Rawley had stepped in behind his blow, however, and he now moved quicker than ever. Fergie saw a glint of steel—he could not have said from where it had come—and then Rawley hit Medlow in the stomach; he then saw that Rawley's hand had been wrapped around a knife and that the blade had disappeared into the man's midsection, entering at a spot just below the breastbone.

Medlow gasped and a horrified look spread over his face when he looked down, seeing Rawley's knife protruding from his abdomen, driven in almost to the hilt. Rawley had reached out with his left hand as he struck, clamping it over Medlow's right so as to prevent him from drawing the pistol; he stood there calmly as he watched the life quickly seep from the man's face and body. Medlow's bones seemed to be turning into jelly. He gradually slumped and then collapsed in a heap. Rawley pulled the knife out with a quick jerk as the man went down; a torrent of dark blood jetted out into the dust.

"We may need all our horses," Rawley said to the silent men, none of whom had moved. "Anyone who abuses a horse or a mule will answer to me. Whoever buries him can have his outfit. Except for his weapons, I mean; those go back into the common supply."

With that he bent down to wipe his blade off on Medlow's shirt-sleeve and then walked away, as cool and calm as Fergie had ever seen him. The men stood around for a moment or two, silently eying the corpse. Then Corto, the dark, sour-looking Indian who had guided them out of San Antonio when they fled to Rawley's camp, stepped forward and announced his desire for Medlow's saddle and boots. No one contested his claim and he went back to the wagons to get himself a shovel.

"That boss man, he sure don't want nobody ruining a horse," Paco muttered when he and Fergie had the herd deployed and on the move. "Never saw nobody so tender-hearted for horses and mules!"

"Yeah, it might be a while before we have that barbecued mule you was talking about," Fergie replied, drawing a brief grin from the man.

Fergie had a very strong suspicion that Rawley's solicitous attitude owed nothing to a love for horses. Rather, he imagined, the man knew that they might need all their mounts, just as he had said, and that a horse or mule unfit for work might very well endanger the success of their expedition. Certainly Rawley had showed no compunction whatever about killing Medlow.

"It's just as well," Tom said when Fergie drew him aside that evening and mentioned the killing. "I've had my eye on that feller the last day or two and I had a notion he might be getting a little restless. The only thing I was wondering was, why'd old Bax wait so long to do the job?"

"Where'd that knife come from?" Fergie asked. "First thing I knew, there it was in that feller's gizzard, just like it had growed there all along."

"He usually keeps one up his sleeve," Tom replied. "And another one in a boot or maybe at the back of his neck. Didn't I tell you he was handy with a knife? I'm telling you, Fergie, he sure ain't nobody to mess around with."

"Well, I reckon everybody'll keep a good, close eye on their saddle blankets from now on. I know I sure flapped mine out good tonight!"

"That's probably one reason why he went for that feller so quick—just to make sure that everybody knew he really meant business. You noticed something peculiar about this outfit of ours? There ain't a one of them Mexicans that has him a pair of them big spurs like you see some of them using sometimes. And them fellers that looks like Indians, you notice how they take such good care of their horses? That's army for you. Old Bax, he ain't forgot none of it, not a bit. In our old outfit mistreating a horse was just about as bad as going to sleep on guard duty."

Fergie said nothing, though he was mentally kicking himself for not having noticed the points his uncle had mentioned. Both Mexicans and Indians had a proverbial reputation for abusing horseflesh, though he had seen very little firsthand evidence to support the claim; the vaqueros he had known in the brush country of the Nueces had always given their horses excellent care, for the most part. Regardless, he made sure that he brushed his own horses down after the day's ride and he shook out his saddle blanket with scrupulous care each night.

Tom rode in to Rawley, who was keeping a position several

yards in front of the lead wagon, late the next morning and said that someone was keeping abreast of them about a mile off to the right. He had caught a glint of sun on metal earlier and, thus alerted, had detected occasional signs of movement in the distance. Rawley listened impassively as they jogged along in front of the wagons.

"Pull your guard post in to about two hundred yards from the wagons," he ordered when Tom had had his say. "If it's more than one person they might mean trouble, and we owe it to ourselves to be in the best position for replying in kind."

He then rode back to the remuda and told Fergie to relay the report to the men riding guard on the opposite side of the wagons; they were also to bring their posts in closer and to be on the alert.

"And, Paco, hold the horses up to within about a hundred yards of the wagons," he added. "If trouble starts we want to have everything fairly well grouped together; they might try picking off the stragglers first."

Nothing happened during the rest of the day, apart from the usual business of covering miles. At first Fergie felt a burst of exhilaration which threatened to burst his chest open when he heard of the distant rider, but after an hour or so, when nothing had happened, the excitement began to wear off and he settled himself down to the humdrum business of keeping the remuda bunched together and close to the wagons.

"There's a jacal about half a mile up there," Corto reported that evening when he had ridden in from his post on the left front of the group. "Looks like somebody's living there."

"Jacal?" Rawley repeated, turning to Tom. "What does he mean?"

Rawley had been taking steps to pick up at least a smattering of Spanish and asked the Spanish equivalent of everything he saw but his progress had necessarily been slow.

"It's a kind of a shack," Tom told him. "Something a really poor family would live in. You run across one stuck out in the brush every once in a while down here. Probably somebody minding a herd of goats or something."

"It's difficult to conceive of this land supporting much life at all," he muttered, looking around at the harsh, brushy land. "Tom, get Biscuit and two more men. We'll ride up there and see if anyone is at home; maybe they can tell us more about the area. Perhaps there are bandits about, who knows? Frenchy, stay here and mount a guard around the wagons. We ought not to be long."

Fergie got out his father's old Spencer when the party had ridden off. Frenchy spotted the old weapon and called out to him.

"You'd better swap that old single shot for one of them new models," he said, jerking a thumb back to the wagons. "Here, we can bust open a box and—hell, there ain't no need for that; you can have Medlow's rifle. It's a brand-new one, too."

He searched through the wagons until he found the dead man's rifle and handed it to the youth. Fergie checked it over, found it in perfect working condition and fully loaded with ammunition.

"You just keep on working that lever and she'll do the rest," Frenchy told him. "Get you a spot picked out over yonder somewhere and look sharp—there might be visitors in the neighborhood pretty soon."

The only sign of human activity they saw, however, was Rawley and his party returning an hour later. They called out when they were well away from the wagons, taking good care to identify themselves, and rode in with plenty of space between themselves. Fergie's ears had caught the lethal sounds of rifle actions being cocked as they had approached; he would not have wanted to try approaching their camp unannounced. He went over to his uncle, who was sitting propped against a wagon wheel, as soon as he had been relieved at his guard post.

"Got you one of them new rifles, huh?" Tom asked, noticing the weapon in his nephew's hands.

"It was . . . that feller that got stuck, it was his," Fergie replied. "Frenchy gave it to me when I was going out to stand guard. Find out anything?"

"It's pretty hard to tell. The old feller living in the jacal, he herds some goats out here. He ain't seen no *bandidos* lately but there's supposed to be a really tough nut around in this neighborhood. Julio Guerra, they call him; he mostly rustles a few cattle and horses but he'll have a go at anything else that looks worthwhile. The old man thought he might have fifteen or twenty men."

"Did he know anything about the country up ahead?"

"That's what's so hard to tell. He thinks there's a big town off to the southwest there someplace, which is about where you'd figure Monclova to be, but he don't know for sure. Poor old soul, I reckon he ain't never been no more than twenty or thirty miles from where he is right now. Anyway, he says there's a road four or five miles up ahead but he don't know where it comes from or goes to. As far as he's concerned the world stops right where the hacienda San Jerónimo ends— that's what we're on right now."

"We ain't figuring on going into Monclova, are we? That's a fair-sized town, ain't it?"

"Thousand or so people, maybe more," Tom acknowledged. "I reckon we'll go to the north of it some and pass it by. It wouldn't be too smart to get too close to a town that big, not with us carrying the load we are and things as uncertain as they are."

"He say anything about the war? Are there any Frenchies around?"

"Huh! He didn't even know there *was* a war! You ought to have seen Bax's face when he started trying to tell that old man what a Frenchman was!"

Fergie had to smile at the thought. He had had occasion to run across men like that in the brush country at home, men who had tended their herds of goats and cattle since childhood and who had lived with their charges so long they sometimes seemed scarcely human. None too sure himself what a Frenchman was—they lived in France, drank a lot of wine and ate snails and frogs, he believed—he could easily imagine Rawley's difficulty.

"You reckon that Guerra outfit might try for the wagons tonight?"

"Not too likely, I'd guess. He's probably got enough Indian

in him that he won't be none too hot on going to war at night. I wouldn't stake my neck on that, though. He's a little more likely to take another day or two to size us up and get his courage worked up good and strong."

"It looks like we're in a pretty good spot," Fergie ventured. "I mean, there ain't no brush or rocks within a hundred yards of the wagons, almost, and with the horses backed up in that little draw over there, it'd be hard to get them stampeded."

"You might notice that Bax generally picks that kind of place for a camp," Tom told him. "Sometimes they ain't much on water or pretty scenery but they're generally pretty good places to fight from."

The night passed peacefully enough. Fergie heard his uncle and another man tell Rawley in the morning that they thought they had detected movement in the brush during the night but had not been certain enough to take any action. Rawley nodded and turned to the group having breakfast. He ordered Cruz and Corto to investigate the report. They returned within the hour and said that two men had scouted through the area, both wearing sandals, but had remained well back in the brush while investigating the camp.

"Ride around and tell everyone to watch carefully," Fergie was told. "It's beginning to look as though they might have a definite interest in us."

Fergie and Paco kept the horses close to the wagons during the day. They made excellent time, due mostly to coming upon the road the old goatherd had mentioned. Since the road ran toward the southwest they took it; although it badly needed repairing in spots, it allowed them to move faster than if they had been moving cross-country.

"Wait till night," Paco said, noticing Fergie's nervousness. "They figure out where we camp, then wait there. They'll be around water, you'll see."

That made good sense, Fergie decided after thinking it over. There were not likely to be many sources of water in the vicinity—they had seen nothing all day to suggest even so much as a spring—and if there were a waterhole up ahead any attacker would be sure to wait there. The nights still had a chill, especially since they had left the flat, brush-infested plain and begun easing upward as they neared the looming mountains in the west, but the days were hot enough to ensure that everyone developed an acute thirst as long as the sun was out.

Rawley halted the train in midafternoon and ordered everyone to assemble near him. Paco motioned for Fergie to attend the meeting, and he rode toward the wagons in a hurry. Tom grinned at him as he rode up beside him and dismounted. Fergie felt very important suddenly, realizing that he was now attending his first council of war.

"If this map is even half accurate," Rawley began, brandishing a rolled-up sheet of paper, "there ought to be a creek or a river a few miles up ahead. I would expect them to wait for us there."

"I was thinking maybe I was seeing a little patch of green up ahead," Biscuit, who had been riding point, said. "Reckon that's what it was."

"Excellent! Then we must bear off to the west," Rawley said. "We'll take our chances on finding a crossing up there; the important thing is to avoid crossing where they might be expecting us. Everyone watch closely, now, and when we get to water we'll pick out the best site and camp there. Stay close to the wagons and be alert at all times."

"Why would he want to go to the west?" Fergie muttered to his uncle when the meeting broke up and they were walking back to their horses. "Why not cut off to the left? You got to figure the country'll be rougher when we move upstream and start getting closer to them mountains."

"If they're waiting at that crossing, and it's likely that they are, then if we go upstream we'll have the sun behind us if they come up after us," Tom explained. "And if you think that don't make a difference, you just try looking one way and then the other about five o'clock this afternoon. And besides, if the country's rougher then that means they'll likely be expecting us to go the other way. It's always the best bet to try doing what the other feller don't expect you to do—gets them off balance and gives you a little more edge."

With that he mounted and rode off to his post. Fergie tried the experiment his uncle had suggested as he rode back to join Paco and the remuda. Looking to the east and southeast, away from the midafternoon sun, he found that he could see normally, but when he squinted into the west he immediately saw the logic behind Rawley's choice. Even though the sun was still high he could see far less clearly; the shadows seemed much thicker and the glare was definitely more annoying. Later in the day, when the sun rested just atop the jagged western skyline, the glare would be almost blinding; anyone coming from the east, he saw, would be squinting into almost total darkness. Fergie's respect for Rawley's sagacity and cunning rose all the higher once he had completed the experiment.

They came upon the river—acutally it was more nearly a creek—an hour before the time they would normally have halted for the day. Rawley had the outriders scout the area thoroughly and, finding it free of bandits, set six men to filling the water kegs as fast as they could. He gave them only twenty minutes in which to replenish their water supplies as much as possible. Then they moved on, finding the creek no barrier at all for the wagons; one of the scouts had found an excellent spot for their camp and they hurried to get there before dark.

Four men stayed at the creek to stand guard while the remuda drank, then helped drive the animals toward camp. Many had not drunk their fill, but Paco shook out a twenty-foot length of his rawhide lariat and used it as a whip with a touch so unerring Fergie could hardly believe what he was seeing. The man allowed a length of riata to drag behind him until he saw a horse or mule hanging back. Then, flicking his wrist and forearm, he brought the lariat whistling forward, snapping it at the last moment to produce a violent pop as the six-inch cracker at the tip popped against the offending animal's flank. The chastened beast needed no repetition to learn the lesson.

"In the morning," Paco said as they walked back to the wagons after turning the herd over to their relief. "They come in the morning. Or maybe they get smart and don't come at all."

Fergie repeated this warning to his uncle later that night. Tom nodded his agreement with the prediction.

"That sounds about right," he said. "We foxed them for tonight, I reckon, but I just hope there ain't some other poor souls trying to use that crossing tonight. Them boys, they might really be hot under the collar when they find out we ain't going to be at their little party after all."

"But in the morning they'll have the sun behind them," Fergie pointed out. "If they decide to come up after us, I mean."

"Sure they will, but we'll be shooting from ground *we* picked out, and that can make a world of difference. Besides, it won't be all that much on their side anyway. You didn't notice anything peculiar about this spot, I reckon?"

Fergie thought for a moment but could not find any unusual characteristics to the spot they had chosen for a camp. They were situated on the edge of a small, level area with almost no vegetation on it. To the east and north of their position, at the edge of the plain, a series of gullies led down to the creek they had crossed, almost as though a gigantic hand had clawed away at the plain and had left deep scratches in the parts it had broken off.

"For one thing they'll have to get across them gullies and come right up that slope in front of us if they come out of the east or north," Tom explained. "And that ain't exactly the best ground in the world to attack from."

Rawley summoned them together as soon as he could that night and announced that he was doubling the guard for that night. Every man would have to pull two shifts of guard duty, he said, and he cautioned them all to be especially alert.

"Every man will be awake and ready from four o'clock on," he added. "Beds rolled and stowed, horses saddled. If they attack, most of us will fight from under the wagons. Biscuit, Frenchy, Tom, you'll form a mobile troop with me. If the time looks ripe we'll charge out to finish them off. And everyone remember this: I want at least one of those scoundrels alive!"

CHAPTER TWELVE

"Shoot at anything that moves," Rawley told the men as he directed them to posts under the wagons. "All our men are inside the wagons or behind them so you need not worry about hitting one of our own!"

Fergie sprawled behind a wagon wheel and shoved his rifle through it, resting the barrel on a spoke. He laid his pistol in his hat and dumped a partial box of cartridges in it too. He could make out the horizon to the east, but the area immediately in front of the wagons was still as dark as it had ever been. After remaining in place for a few minutes without moving, the early-morning chill began seeping through his coat and he wished he had had the foresight to have brought a blanket for a pallet.

Cruz, nestled behind the front wheel of the same wagon, lay on a thick, multihued woolen poncho. Tom and the others forming the mounted reserve were off to the right rear, out of sight; Fergie realized that he would feel much more at ease if his uncle were beside him and he cursed himself for such childish notions.

"Sssstt!"

Someone to his left had hissed the warning. The broken, sloping area in front of the wagons had grown steadily lighter in the twenty or so minutes they had been in place. Fergie could make out the dim outlines of boulders and century plants on the slope but he could see nothing moving.

He happened to be looking directly at a century plant, a dark and jagged clump with a spear reaching twenty feet into the air, when he saw a blossom of brilliant orange flame appear just above the pointed leaves. For a second the phenomenon befuddled him; the sound of a rifle bellowing brought him to life and he then knew that he had seen his first hostile gunfire.

"Godamighty, he's close!" he muttered, levering a round into the chamber of his rifle.

He drew a careful bead on the plant, which was no more than sixty yards off, and fired two quick rounds, aiming low and to either side of its center. Firing broke out all along the line of wagons, along with intermittent whoops and cries. Blossoms of gunfire dotted the slope below them and he heard a bullet thump into the wagon above his head.

"Gringo bastard! I'll eat your guts for breakfast!" someone below yelled out in Spanish.

"Come close enough to try for 'em and I'll have yours for a hatband!" Cruz answered, punctuating his promise with a blast from his rifle.

Additional threats and insults volleyed up from the attackers, drawing ample reply in kind from those defenders who understood Spanish. Fergie tried hard to find something moving to serve as a target but he could not; he instead began spotting gun muzzle blasts in front of him and directing his answering fire at those spots. It became clear very quickly that there were not many attackers, or perhaps they were more careful with their ammunition; at any rate the volume of fire from under the wagons was at least three or four times that coming from the slope below them.

"Yeee-hawwwww!"

Fergie looked to the right, recognizing his uncle's cry, and saw the four of them spurring down the slope. They rode bent low in their saddles, pistols in hand, and charged directly at the advancing bandits. Cruz called out to him to hold his fire but he had already dropped the Spencer from his shoulder, marveling at the ferocity of the charge. He saw Rawley guide his horse directly toward a bandit who had reared up from behind a clump of prickly pear, rifle swinging to his shoulder; Rawley fired from no more than ten feet away and the bandit went down as though he had been struck by a gigantic hammer.

Tom and his three companions completed a sweep in quick order and rode back up onto the shelf where the wagons stood. Tom spotted a single bandit retreating to the northeast and set out at a gallop after him, unslinging his rope on the run. The man had thrown away his rifle and darted through the low underbrush like a startled deer, zigzagging furiously. Tom's horse, trained for years in the fine art of chasing down yearlings in much thicker brush, easily caught up with the man and skidded to a halt when it sensed the throw of the loop. The noose settled neatly over the darting man; Tom jerked it closed and leaped down, palming his pistol on the run.

Fergie saw the man jerked from his feet with his arms firmly pinned to his sides by the rope. Tom ran up to him and stuck his pistol in the man's face. Before turning his attention back to the scene directly in front of him, Fergie saw his uncle hustle his captive back to his feet and direct him toward the waiting trio of Biscuit, Frenchy and Rawley. Upon inspecting the slope, he saw three or four figures darting away in the distance, easily three or four hundred yards off.

"Hey, they didn't like our little fiesta!" Cruz cackled. "Hell, they're supposed to be such bad *hombres?* My kid brother could make them run for home!"

"I-i-is it all over and done with?" Fergie asked, finding that he had to swallow hard several times in order to clear a strange dryness out of his throat before he could speak.

"Probably, but don't stand up in front of the wagons," Cruz warned. "One or two might be down there yet, just hoping to pick somebody off. Let's us just lay here and see what happens next."

Biscuit, Rawley and Frenchy rode down the slope again, proceeding at a walk with their pistols drawn and ready. Biscuit stopped, dismounted and stooped over a crumpled figure. He drew a knife, slashed at the man's throat and moved on after picking up a rifle that lay beside him.

"Let them finish off whoever might be alive down there," Cruz said, reaching into his shirt for his tobacco. "I damned near got myself shot good one time by a man who was already supposed to be dead."

"Are . . . are they going to kill all of them?" Fergie asked, taken aback at the cold-blooded slaughter he saw taking place before him.

"Huh? Sure they are!" Cruz said, surprised at the question. "Hell, we sure ain't going to doctor them, not after they tried so hard to plant us!"

Fergie twisted around to look at his uncle, who was marching his prisoner toward the wagons. The man wore a ragged shirt and even more ragged trousers, both of the white cotton favored by natives of the region, and he stumbled as he advanced. Fergie noticed that he was holding his right arm tenderly and then he saw a dark splotch on the man's right sleeve.

Rawley and the others covered the slope, making sure that not a single bandit remained alive, and then rode up to the wagons. They had a collection of rifles and pistols, all percussion models, and dumped them into the back of a wagon before dismounting. Biscuit was wiping his knife on the leg of his trousers as he rode up.

"Aha! A little pigeon!" Cruz murmured, turning and for the first time seeing Tom and his prisoner. "Now we have some fun, I bet!"

The men came out from under the wagons, laughing and obviously relieved at having come out of the attack with no casualties among themselves. Good-humored arguments broke out as they began proclaiming how many bandits they had killed, each man claiming to have slain every corpse on the slope.

"How many you kill?" Cruz asked Fergie, grinning with anticipation.

"I don't know," the youth replied, averting his eyes. "Not any, I reckon."

He had watched the century plant which had blossomed into gunfire to signal the start of the battle, but he had not seen any sign of a body near it.

"Just slip them knives back into your belts," Tom said as he rode up, prisoner in tow. He repeated his warning in Spanish, making his voice a little sharper. "You know what Rawley said," he added, "he wanted one bandit alive and this is the one."

Rawley rode up and dismounted at that moment. He

looked at the captive, said nothing and turned back to his men. He ordered the teamsters to get their mules harnessed and prepared to move. The others were to assume their regular duties.

"We'll keep him with us for a while," he said, gesturing to the prisoner. "Tom, tell him to use part of his shirt to wrap his arm up if he wants to. Then put a rope around his neck and tie the other end to the back of the lead wagon. Tell him that I will have his skin if he tries to unfasten the rope."

Tom translated the orders into Spanish. The man, who looked to be about thirty and in no way different from any field laborer or goatherd to be seen in the area, shrugged and began ripping off the right sleeve of his shirt. He wrapped it around his arm, folding the ends under in lieu of making a knot—no one offered to help him—and assumed his place behind the wagon. A teamster knotted a rope around his neck and then to the wagon's tailgate, giving him about fifteen feet of slack. He stood there patiently, seemingly ready for whatever might come and fully resigned to his fate.

"What do you reckon Rawley'll do with that feller?" Fergie asked Paco when they had the horse herd under way and were riding side by side.

"I don't know, but I wouldn't want to be him! Maybe he let us use him for target practice, huh? Or maybe we throw knives at him? Yes, that man, it's all over with for him. He'll see his momma and poppa and all the saints before very long, I bet on that!"

Fergie shivered again. The cold-blooded way Rawley and his men had gone about killing the few bandits who were not already dead had made him very ill at ease, but Paco's eagerness to dispose of the prisoner in ways which Fergie thought more suitable for Indians turned his stomach completely. He resolved that he would have nothing to do with torturing the prisoner if it came to that. Riding out to one edge of the remuda, mostly to get away from Paco, he realized that the man had not shown any hatred for the prisoner while he was proposing various ways to end his days on earth; Paco seemed to consider the prospect an interesting one, but vengeance did not appear to figure among his motives.

"Sure, it's a bad business," Tom agreed when Fergie expressed his feelings that evening. "It's just like I was telling you, boy: that Bax is a mighty tough, mean customer and them that gets crossways with him had better watch their step. Biscuit and Frenchy, they're just as bad in their way, except they ain't so smart about it."

"What do you reckon he's going to do with that one?" Fergie asked, sneaking a look toward their prisoner. The man sat quietly in the dust behind the wagon, still tied to it.

"I wouldn't even begin to guess. But I'll tell you one thing —I wouldn't be in that poor soul's place for nothing in the world! You can bet that whatever it is, he won't like it a bit. And like as not it'll be something that'll help us get to where we're going a little easier. Bax might be a mean, cold-blooded bastard—hell, they ain't no 'might be' about that!—but I'll say this for him: he won't bother with hurting nobody unless he stands to gain something out of it. But if he does, look out! There ain't nobody he won't do in!"

"But you make him sound like . . . well, like some kind of animal!"

"There just might be something to that," Tom agreed, looking thoughtful for a moment as he considered Fergie's remark at face value. "Yep, I reckon you could say that Bax is something about like a rattler, say. They'll lay there all coiled up, you know, snoozing away real peaceful and enjoying the sunshine like nobody's business. But you just step close to him and then, watch out! Except there never was a rattler that could look ahead and scheme and all like old Bax can."

"It was pretty slick, the way he missed that crossing on purpose and come on up to that other spot," Fergie said after a short silence. "I guess it would have been a lot harder on us if we'd have tried bulling our way across down there where they was waiting."

"You just might have something there. Hell, we didn't even get nobody so much as grazed! And there was eight of them laying out there when we rode off. They wasn't so much, to have had such a bad name; you know they was all carrying old percussion rigs? Damnedest mess of odds and ends you ever saw for a gang of outlaws. It's a wonder some of them old pieces would fire at all."

Fergie noticed that someone was getting up from the circle of men around Rawley and going over to the prisoner. He watched closely, fearing that they were going to begin torturing the captive, but then saw the man—he identified him as Cruz—hand the prisoner a sack of food and a canteen, which he eagerly accepted. Tom nudged his nephew and nodded toward the pair.

"Old Bax is sure enough fattening him up for something," he said. "I reckon we'll just have to sit back and see what for when the time comes."

No one had paid any attention to the prisoner once it had become clear that Rawley wanted him kept alive and unharmed. Neither did anyone go out of his way to make the man especially comfortable, Fergie also noticed; he curled up beneath the wagon to which he was tied and spent the night there without a blanket.

They came upon a small settlement in the middle of the following day. The scout in front had ridden back to report the presence of a village to Rawley. After learning that it had only twenty houses at most, far too few to be honored by the presence of a military garrison, Rawley ordered his men to aim directly for it.

"Go on in, see the town," Paco said to Fergie when they had moved the horses down to a broad plain near the cluster of houses. "I seen places like that before; ain't nothing new there for me."

Fergie took him at his word and turned his horse toward the village. The wagons were drawn up side by side at the edge of the settlement; most of the men were already wandering among the houses. The place did not have a street in the proper sense of the word. Each house had been sited exactly where the builder had felt like putting it, and no two of the builders had agreed on the proper orientation. The result was a hodgepodge of houses and huts, all facing in different directions and interconnected by a maze of well-worn footpaths. If there was a focus to the place it was the well, situated in the approximate center of the dwellings.

Rawley stood beside the well, flanked by Tom, Frenchy and four more of his men. Fergie rode up nearby and dismounted. There was not a single villager to be seen, though this did not fool the youth; well acquainted with the ways of backcountry dwellers, he knew that every eye in the village was trained on them from within the houses.

"It ain't so much of a much," Biscuit grunted in disgust. "Easy to see why they wouldn't waste no troops on protecting this place!"

The buildings were of the simplest, rudest construction. The most popular building style called for the planting of a series of posts in a rectangle the size of the projected house. Branches, stripped of leaves and twigs, were woven in and out in a horizontal pattern among those uprights, rather like the willow baskets Fergie had seen many a man make in his spare time; the craftsman left a blank spot for a door and in a few cases the resulting wattle had been daubed with a mixture of mud and straw. Longer branches laid across the open top, covered with brush, served as a roof of sorts. Some of the huts had a skin draped across the opening which served for a doorway, but most had nothing at all. The houses were all of the same color as the dirt or wood that had served as the building material, and consequently they looked almost as if the earth itself had humped up into a houselike form.

Chickens ran freely through the village, darting in and out of doorways. No other animal life was to be seen, though Fergie could hear a pig snuffling somewhere. Upon looking the village over more closely, he saw three houses made of adobe bricks, and one, the largest, had a partial covering of mud plaster as well as a hole that could have been called a window. The latter house also had a real door, a poorly fitted affair made of imperfectly hewn planks, leaving plenty of gaps. It was the only house in the village that looked as though it might have more than one room, though neither of its compartments could have been more than eight or ten feet square.

It had a pen, made of cholla branches stacked to form a thickly barbed fence, straggling off to one side of the house. All the houses had brush-covered *ramadas* nearby; Fergie suspected that a great deal of the villagers' lives took place under those open sheds.

"The place certainly looks poor enough to be virtuous," Rawley remarked.

"Don't let that fool you none," Tom cautioned. "Some of them *bandidos* we seen might have come from right here. It don't look like the pickings at home would have been very much; I'll have to go that far with you."

"Call out for their mayor, or whatever their head man might be called," Rawley said. "Ask him to come here."

"*Dónde es el jefe?*" Tom called out. "*Su alcalde? Venga aquí!*"

There was no response. Rawley pointed to the largest house and told Frenchy to bring out its inhabitants. He advanced to the house, pistol in hand, and pushed open the door. Looking inside, he motioned with his pistol and then stepped back to allow a small procession to emerge. First came an old man, fat and almost white-haired, except for a few black strands; then came three women of various ages and two small children wearing only shirts that hung to their knees. The old man put on a ragged straw hat when he stepped out into the sun. He shuffled forward in response to Rawley's beckoning finger. Fergie saw that he was wearing sandals, strips of rawhide cut to fit the soles of his gnarled feet, more or less, and held in place by a network of thongs. The women and children were barefooted.

"Ask him if he's the chief," Rawley said.

Tom did so and was told that the *jefe* was not there that day.

"He's probably lying," Tom said after he had translated for Rawley. "Most likely he figures we're going to plunder the town and kill the *jefe* on general principles."

"Then tell him that we mean no harm to any of his people," Rawley said. "We have our own food and water and we want only one thing from him, a guide to show us the way to the other side of the mountains, to the west. Tell him that I'll pay the guide . . . oh, ten dollars, silver."

Rawley took a pouch from his coat pocket and counted out ten silver dollars while Tom spoke. Fergie saw the old man's eyes narrow slightly when he noticed the big silver coins flashing in Rawley's hand.

"He still says the *jefe* ain't here and there ain't no way across the mountains," Tom said when the old man again had replied.

"Frenchy, Biscuit, Corto, gather up some more men and go through all those shacks," Rawley called out. "I want them emptied in three minutes! And while they're doing that, Tom, you can tell the old man this: I don't believe that there is not at least one man in the village who doesn't know his way across those mountains. I have offered to pay good money for assistance, but if he wishes to be stubborn then I will have a guide in another way."

The old man listened impassively as Tom translated for him. Fergie went to the nearest hut and looked inside. For a moment he could see nothing at all; there were no windows and by standing in the doorway he blocked off most of the little light penetrating the small room. Then his eyes grew more accustomed to the darkness and he saw a woman crouched in the farthest corner, holding three small children against her body. He asked her to step outside, promising that they would not be hurt, and then escorted them to the group already forming beside the well.

The old man still had not spoken when all of the villagers had been assembled in the dust around him. There was a fair sprinkling of men in the crowd, though not nearly enough to match up with all the women, and rather fewer children than one would have expected. Rawley glanced around at all of them before asking Tom to translate his next speech to them.

"We are from Texas, on our way to the west, and we do not intend to rob you or to destroy your village. We have asked this old man to point out your chief and to recommend some-one to act as our guide through those mountains. We will pay the guide ten dollars in silver; I have the money here.

Does anyone wish to tell me who is the chief? Can anyone guide us through the mountains?"

There was a short, low buzz of conversation as the villagers exchanged furtive words, but no one stepped forward to answer Rawley's questions. The old man surveyed the villagers and seemed to find a certain measure of satisfaction in their continued reticence.

"Very well, we must proceed to alternative measures," Rawley announced. "In one minute, if no one speaks, I will have one of my men shoot one of you dead!"

Fergie sucked in his breath but could not make himself move. He had heard that calm, knife-edged tone in Rawley's voice before; he had spoken in exactly the same way a moment before killing Medlow. Rawley took his watch from his pocket, flipped open the case and studied it elaborately as Tom translated the warning. After a short wait he looked over at Corto, who stood beside the old man.

"Shoot one of the children," Rawley ordered. "Take that one first!"

He pointed to a child, a scrawny imp who might have been six years old; Fergie gaped mindlessly for a moment before recognizing the woman to whom the child clung—she was the woman he had brought from her hut. Before he could move or make a sound, Corto had pulled the child away from his mother, drawn his pistol and fired a round into the scrawny, twisting body. The bullet flung the child into a limp, huddled mass of rags and bones. The woman screamed, a gut-wrenching sound of agony, and fell to her knees beside the child.

"If no one speaks in another minute I will have two children shot, and in the minute after that, three," Rawley called out, unmoved by the woman's grief and as calm as he had ever been. "I am willing to shoot everyone in this village. But you, old man, you will be the last to die!"

He looked down again at his watch as Tom began translating the grim warning. Fergie staggered over to his horse and leaned against the animal's shoulder. He had never before heard of anyone killing helpless children, unless maybe it was the Comanches; the sight of the child being flung backward by the heavy bullet, as well as the loud grief of the woman, sickened him to the core.

"*Diga!*" "*Cabrón!*" "*Diga, viejo!*"

The angry cries of the villagers welled up, forcing him to turn around. Before Corto could begin shooting again one of the women stepped out of the crowd and pointed a trembling finger at the old man.

"There he is, he is the *jefe*," she screamed, her face distorted with rage. "The old billygoat, he's the one! Tell them what they want to know, you old fool, or I will kill you myself!"

"How about it, *viejo?*" Tom asked, drawing his pistol and tracing a design with its muzzle on the front of the old man's dirty shirt. "We got lots of bullets but we wouldn't waste one on you! No, for you I think we'd have something special. Maybe we'd just cut off your eyelids and then stake you out on the ground so you could look up at the sun till you went blind. And we'd be damned sure that that woman stayed alive awhile too; she might enjoy seeing you on your way to hell!"

The tone of barely controlled ferocity in Tom's voice frightened even Fergie, who had never seen his uncle in such a state. Corto looked over to Rawley for instructions. Rawley held up a restraining finger as he watched the old man. The *jefe* gnawed his lip for a moment, looking both sad and angry, but he could see that whatever authority he had among the villagers was evaporating by the second. He bowed his head and spoke.

"There is a pass through a canyon a day's journey south of here," he admitted. "The Indians use it when they come down from the north in the fall. Hilario can show you the way."

Hilario stepped out of the crowd, hat in hand and eyes downcast. The villagers started back to their houses but Rawley stopped them.

"Bring our prisoner out," he called to a man standing near the wagons.

When the captive had been marched into the center of

the improvised arena, Rawley again addressed the people through Tom. Another buzz of furtive talk had run through the villagers when they saw the man; Tom had to raise his voice to make himself heard as he translated.

"This man was part of a group of bandits who tried to attack us yesterday morning," Rawley began. "We killed eight of them, took this one alive and chased the others as far as they could run. I will now show you what happens to those who try attacking me or my men or my wagons."

With that he reached out and took a rifle from the man standing closest to him. He turned to the prisoner, reversed the rifle with a quick flip and drove the butt into his stomach. The prisoner collapsed, gagging for breath; as he lay writhing upon the ground Rawley raised the rifle high and plunged the butt down upon the man's right ankle. He struck the ankle three times as hard as he could; Fergie could hear bones crunching and snapping as the heavy, iron-plated rifle butt descended again and again. Rawley then turned his attention to the left ankle and demolished it in the same way. After that he broke the man's hands, carefully pinning a wrist down with his boot to get a stationary target.

The crowd watched in silence as he completed the brutal deed. The captive cried out once, as the first blow descended against his ankle, and then lapsed into a bubbling, incoherent wail. When Rawley had completed his work, he tossed the rifle back to its owner and stepped back.

"You can feed him or kill him or care for him, whatever you like," he said. "We are on our way. If you have friends or relatives who are bandits, tell them to stay away from us unless they want to die!"

With that he motioned for Hilario to follow him. He turned away from the villagers, led his horse and Hilario back to the wagons and mounted, calling out to Fergie to bring a horse for their guide. When Fergie glanced over his shoulder at the village for the last time, he saw a crowd of women gathered around the child Corto had shot; that sight stayed with him for a long time afterward.

CHAPTER THIRTEEN

Hilario proved to be an adequate guide. Rawley put him on a horse and directed Tom to take him to the point, where he could guide the wagons into the best route for getting them across the mountains. Hilario said nothing for several hours, obviously unsure of the party's intentions toward him, but that evening he loosened up once he had received a cup of hot coffee and his portion of the pinole, jerky and pemmican which served them all for a meal.

"Don Federico, he will be a very sad man this night," he said to Tom, whom he had grown to trust somewhat. "He might not even be our *jefe* any longer."

"Oh? Why's that?" Tom asked, deducing that the old, fat man's name had been Don Federico.

"That man whose hands and feet your leader broke, you remember him? That was Pascual, Don Federico's grandson," Hilario explained. "He is a very bad man, a part of Julio Guerra's band of robbers and murderers. If anyone in the village said or did anything to displease Don Federico, that man received a visit from Pascual himself when the bandits rode into the village. He has killed many, many men, that one, and violated many a poor woman. Now Don Federico will no longer have anyone to do his killing for him."

"Hey, how about that for good luck?" Tom chuckled, nudging Fergie, who sat beside him. "And I bet you was thinking that we'd done something just awful, and here it turns out that maybe we fixed it up so that them villagers could get out from under Don Federico's fat, dirty thumb!"

"It might look that way now," Fergie retorted, breaking out of a long silence, "but that wasn't why he done what he did and you know it!"

"No, you're right there," Tom conceded. "Old Bax, he don't never go very far out of his way for nobody. It wouldn't have made a bit of difference to him whether that old man was St. Peter's uncle or the Devil hisself! And killing that little kid, that was a pretty rank thing to do, I can't deny that."

"Lordy, that was the worst of all!" Fergie muttered, struggling to keep his voice under control; Rawley was sitting only twenty feet away and he did not want the man to hear what he was saying. "Uncle Tom, I was the one who got that kid's momma out of her house. I told her she wouldn't get hurt; I said there wasn't nothing to worry about! And just look at what he went and done!"

"Aw, hell, Fergie, there wasn't no way for you to know what Bax had in mind," Tom mumbled. "For that matter I didn't know myself. But I guess he figured that they'd worry more about their kids than . . . hell's afire, boy, I done forgot something! You know, come to think of it, I reckon I was about as much to blame for that mess as you. Why, it wasn't no more than a couple or three days ago that I was telling Bax about Mexicans and their kids. You know, about how they set such a store by the young ones? Damn my soul to hell, I sure never thought he'd put it to that kind of use!"

"Well, I reckon I can see now what you meant about him being so all-fired mean," Fergie muttered. "He really would have gone ahead and killed just about everybody in that whole village, wouldn't he?"

"You're mighty right he would! And he wouldn't never lose so much as a wink of sleep over it, neither. Look, Fergie, I can tell you right now the way he looks at it. You might not agree with his way of thinking but it *does* make sense, sort of. See, he figures he owes it to us, as well as to hisself, to get us to where we're going with the least amount of fuss and bother, and to do it as quick as he can. So, if it comes down to a choice between shooting him thirty or forty Mexicans and putting us in a hot spot, you can be damned sure that he's going to start shooting! In a way we'll all be profiting by what he done back there, not that that makes it any the easier to swallow, not by a long shot!"

"I don't think it makes me feel one whit better," Fergie replied. "I just about died when I seen which one of them kids he'd picked out to shoot."

Tom said nothing for a moment. He looked toward his nephew, squinting in the dusk as if to see him better. He could see that the youth was highly agitated.

"You damned little ninny, you think it would have been a bit better if it had been some other little kid?" he finally asked, his voice low but quivering with anger. "What in hell are you *really* worrying about, anyway? The kid or yourself? Hell, every blessed one of them kids had a right to live! You ain't upset because some snotty-nosed little brat got hisself blowed to heaven a lot sooner than usual; you're just wound up because Bax made you out to be a liar! Get on out where you're supposed to be and stand your guard—you're making me sick with all that whining!"

Fergie put down his coffee cup, wrenched himself to his feet and stalked away, his cheeks and ears burning. At first he wanted to pounce on his uncle, to drive him into the dust and pound him into silence, but even in his hottest anger he knew better than to try such a foolhardy move. Instead, he walked away to his guard post, where he spent the next two hours fuming and cursing to himself. He made sure that he unrolled his blankets well away from his uncle that night and he lay in them for a long time before going to sleep. When he awoke the next morning he drank his coffee and ate his pinole by himself and then walked off to saddle his horse without speaking to his uncle, whom he carefully but ostentatiously avoided. Tom's harsh words continued to burn into his brain, however, and at the end of the day he could no longer put off the task he had to perform.

"Uncle Tom," he began, approaching his uncle as he dismounted and began unsaddling after riding in from his patrol, "I . . . I reckon you was right. About me, I mean; I reckon I *was* thinking mostly about myself yesterday. It wasn't no way to be."

"Aw, it ain't no big thing, at least not the arguing part. And hell, you was mostly right anyway. I'm right sorry I flew off the handle at you that way. There wasn't no call to get all huffed up like that."

"No, you was right all the way," Fergie insisted.

"Well, at least maybe you're learning that there ain't nothing so grand about war and killing and all like that. It *was* a mean thing, killing that kid like that, but what was we to do about it? I'm telling you for sure, Fergie: if you'd have got in front of him while he was all heated up back there, he'd have gone right over you like a bull waltzing over a tumblebug!"

"Probably so, but it seems like there ought to have been something I could have done to make it up to that poor woman."

"Like what? Short of raising the kid up from the dead, I mean? Hell, you could even let her shoot you back but that wouldn't give her the kid back, now would it? No, it was a rotten, sorry thing to do and I reckon we'll all have to live with it for a long while. It's the sort of thing you just can't undo, no matter what."

Fergie wrestled with that observation for a moment or two but could make no headway in finding an argument against it.

"I reckon I was pretty far off about that *bandido* too," he finally said. "About feeling sorry for him, I mean. But damn, he sure didn't look like a mean, ornery sort once you had him in your rope!"

"What would Bax or any of these boys look like if you took their knives and guns away from them and tied them up like hens going off to market?"

"Well, one thing's pretty clear: if that Pascual lives he sure won't be bothering anybody else. Them hands and ankles of his, they looked like they was all ruined."

"No, he won't be much trouble to anybody," Tom agreed. "Not unless he can find somebody else to do his meanness for him. And from what Hilario says about the way he's been rubbing them people's faces into the dirt, I wouldn't be surprised if they didn't just finish him off. And maybe Don Federico too, while they're at it!"

Later that night Tom walked out to join his nephew as he stood his turn of guard duty. Fergie started at the sound of someone approaching; it was the first time anyone had come near him during any of his patrols, except for his relief, and he said as much.

"That's the way it is with standing guard duty," Tom replied. "You'll go a month or six weeks and not see a blessed thing, maybe. But that once, boy, that's when you really need somebody out here watching close!"

"It's a shame you can't tell which time it's going to be, so's everybody could be sleeping all them other times."

"Yep, just like it's a shame every day ain't Christmas! But that's the way it is with soldiering, boy: mostly it's just sitting around waiting for something to happen but hoping it don't. But that ain't the reason I come strolling out here. What I had in mind was, well, you remember when we bailed out of San Antonio, how we was just going to stay overnight with Bax and his boys?"

"I remember. Lordy, that seems like it was last year. What was it really, about two weeks ago?"

"About that. Seemed like one thing just led to another and we never did get to split off and go our own way. I was hoping we might could do it once we got across the river, but hell, it didn't seem right to go off and leave them boys out there in the middle of nowhere, especially not with that feller tracking us off to the side like he was doing. So, here we are. What I mean to say is, it looks to me like we're going to have to fish or cut bait here pretty soon. Are we going to stick with these boys or head off down toward Monclova or Monterrey or someplace like that on our own?"

"Mmm, I sure don't know what to say about that. What would we do off down that way?"

"That's a point and a mighty thoughtful one," Tom said. "On the other hand, if we was to go on with Bax and the others, I don't mind telling you it could turn into a ring-tailed doozey before we get it done. I was talking to Hilario a while this morning about what's on the other side of them mountains. He didn't know too much about what's out there, but he ain't never heard nothing good about it. Well, there ain't many Indians, which is something for it, but then that's mostly because there ain't no water, so there's a mighty black mark against it."

"So it figures on being a pretty rough old road, huh?"

"About as bad as any you or me either one ever saw. But that ain't the worst of it; I figure that if people have gone that way before then you and me can make it too. No, what worries me most of all is this bunch Bax has got with him. I got me a mighty strong feeling that some of us ain't going to be around for payday."

"Huh? What do you mean by that?"

"You ain't been paying attention to how some of them boys have been acting up lately? You ain't seen nothing funny going on around here?"

"I reckon not. But then I don't get to see a lot of anybody; me and Paco, we stick pretty close to the horses during the day. And then by the time I get the horses settled down it's time to grab some supper and then it's my turn for guard duty and after that I'm about ready for bed."

"Well, I can tell you straight out there's almost been a couple of fights yesterday and today. And the kind of people these are, it won't be just a scuffling—when they go at it there'll be knives flying and pistols popping, so when something busts loose you'd do best to get into the brush and stay there. Keep your head down and let them fools fight it out of their systems, which is just exactly what I aim to do!"

"What does Rawley think about it?"

"He's just purely fit to be tied," Tom muttered. "But what the hell *can* he do? If he tries to stick his oar in before they get to fighting, he'll have both of them dead set against him, and if he waits, well, it'll be too late by then. This is just about the first time I ever seen old Bax boxed in this way, and I tell you for a fact, if it wasn't so likely to get serious in a hurry I'd bust a gut laughing about it all."

"Why does he have to worry about it anyway? If a couple of hotheads want to slice each other up, what's it going to hurt the rest of us? Unless they happen to wing somebody else, I mean? I just don't see how it's so important."

"You can count it out for yourself," Tom said. "How many of us are there, altogether?"

"Uh, twelve," Fergie replied after pausing to count up all the men. "Or thirteen, if you count Hilario."

"You needn't to count him; I don't think he's likely to know all that much about handling a gun. Now, there's five turns of guard duty, right? We start about seven and go two hours at a turn, two men to a turn. Bax, he don't take a turn because for one thing he's the boss and for another he's up and down all night anyway, checking on everybody and seeing to things hisself."

"That's right," Fergie agreed. "You know, I don't think I ever saw him in his bedroll?"

"He don't sleep much, never did. Damnedest feller ever I seen for staying up and prowling about at night. It don't seem to hurt him none, so don't get yourself lathered up on that score. And Paco, he's up and down all night too, going out to see about them horse-cousins of his, so he don't take a turn neither."

"He sure does seem to like them horses about as well as he likes the rest of us. Even better, maybe. I heard him talking to his horse this morning; he sounded sort of nice, for a change."

"Anyhow, we got us ten guard slots and ten men to fill them," Tom continued. "Now if a couple of damned fools was to shoot each other, or carve each other up so bad they was all laid up, that'd put a real crimp in things. Some of us would have to double up on guard duty and that's real bad. Them that gets picked to go double, they feel like they're working more than the others, which they are, and losing that extra sleep, it makes them testier than ever. With a bunch of tough nuts like the ones Bax has got together here, it wouldn't be long before there was some fights and then you'd be right back in the same hole but a lot deeper."

"In other words it just goes from bad to worse, huh?"

"That's it in a nutshell, Fergie, and I ain't lying a bit. I seen it happen back when I was soldiering and I know for a fact that it's mighty bad business all the way around."

"Well, what are you thinking about doing, then? You reckon maybe we ought to pull out and go it on our own? It seems to me that the way you're talking, you've got *us* boxed in pretty good, too!"

"That's about the size of it and I don't like it one little bit, not no part of it. But I'll be dried and fried if I know what to do. Come to that, I ain't even sure Bax would let us go, the way he's liable to be needing men soon. Anyhow, I just want to let you know why we're still here and not cutting off somewhere else on our own, the way we talked about before. It's just because I flat don't know what else to do, that's all. I don't know when I been in such a spot."

"Well, why don't we just stick with them a while longer?" Fergie suggested. "And it ain't because I'm so wild about it that I say that, neither. But there just ain't nothing for us to do in Monterrey or down that way; it seems to me we'd do better if we was to head over to Chihuahua and then maybe slant north from there if it still looks like we ought to pull out. At least, we'd be closer to New Mexico or someplace like that."

"Yes, and if we stayed long enough to get them rifles delivered we'd have us a right nice little poke to start out with, too. How much money you got left?"

"Ten, fifteen dollars, I reckon."

"And I got maybe twice that. Damn, I wish now we had what we left with that banker! All right, I reckon you're right—let's stick with Bax awhile longer, at least till it starts to looking too rough to stand it. It ain't a good way to do, just blundering along from pillar to post thisaway, but I swear I can't see no other way. I'll tell Bax we're staying for a while the next time I see him."

Rawley smiled and nodded encouragingly when Tom told him that they had decided to stick with him and his crew for the time being. He warned that he could not pay them their wages until he had delivered the rifles; his own stock of coin had sunk perilously low and might be needed before they reached their rendezvous and handed over the rifles.

"That's all right," Tom told him. "We'd likely be going that way anyhow, and at least we'll be getting some free food and protection along the way. I reckon that's worth a good deal."

"Unless some of these fools begin fighting and put each other out of action," Rawley noted. "We're getting down to the bone as far as men are concerned. I'd have preferred having two or three more when we left San Antonio but I couldn't find anyone I trusted. As it was I had to take along a few I'd almost rather have done without. Starting with that fool Medlow, of course."

"That Red, him and Mando or Pilón are going to get into it one of these days too if they don't watch out," Tom warned.

"That will be the end of Red! That Pilón might not be very large but what there is of him is concentrated quickness. He'd have Red's heart out before he knew what happened. And that Mando has a certain air about him too—they both strike me as vicious enough for anyone's taste."

"I ain't ready to start chewing on either one of them," Tom agreed.

Pilón, a skinny mite of a man and without a doubt the dirtiest, most nondescript-looking member of the entire crew, could not have been more than three or four inches over five feet tall. Despite his lack of size and his ragged, filthy clothing he walked with an exaggerated strut; he reminded Fergie mostly of a rooster his mother had once had, a mangy, scruffy bird which had pranced around the chicken coop as though he were the king of all creation. Red stood at least a foot taller and could easily have weighed twice as much as Pilón. Mando, a teamster like Red and Pilón, was tall for a Mexican—with another inch or two he would have been six feet tall—and was also extremely thick and powerful looking. Red attempted to dominate them, clearly regarding them as inferior creatures and trying at every chance to work his wagon into line ahead of them. More than once his bull-headed determination to be in front of them had led directly to barely averted accidents; Rawley had finally put a stop to that jockeying for position by decreeing that Red would drive at the head of the train one day and at the tail of it the next, with Pilón and Mando taking the opposite end from him.

Hilario had directed them back to the northwest once he had found the canyon he wanted. Some of the men complained about having to turn away from the straight-line path to their target, but even Fergie could see that there was no way to avoid the detour. The entire chain of mountains most nearly resembled a series of big, rock-crusted ridges running in a northwest-southeast direction. A few of the ridges were spaced far enough apart to allow more or less open valleys to run between them, but most of these were broken up by cross canyons or massive piles of rock or both.

"Looks just like some giant's playpen," Biscuit said one evening as they sat around the fire eating their meal. "Wonder how it is that all of a sudden you come up onto a big pile of rocks like that one back yonder? Some of them boogers was bigger'n the wagons!"

"It's just nature's way of making it up to you," Frenchy explained, adopting a very serious tone. "It's because she's so blamed stingy with grass and water, you see? So, she just goes overboard and gives you an extra big helping of rocks. It's just plain ungrateful for you to go on about it like that, I swear it is!"

"I never could stand for people to give me things I didn't want nor ask for," Biscuit growled amidst the howls of laughter greeting Frenchy's "explanation," "and that sure does go for cock 'n bull stories like the one I just now heard!"

Contrary to what he had heard and expected, Fergie discovered that the sierra was not entirely waterless. He could see signs of water drainage left over from the last rain, which had certainly not been a recent one; rushing waters had scoured innumerable gullies into the sandy floor of the valley and had uprooted some of the scant vegetation. Hilario showed them how to spot animal trails leading up into the rocks. Many of them, he explained to Tom, led to a *tinaja*, or a natural depression scoured into the rock, and many of them held water, at least for a portion of the year.

Rawley took the lesson to heart and laid down an order that every such trail should be investigated; if it led to a *tinaja* containing water, the caravan was to stop in order for the men to refill as many of the kegs as possible. He admitted that taking these measures would slow their march, but he said that it would be much better to move slowly with water than to move quickly without it; the latter course would soon result in no progress at all and death for all of them.

"Better safe than sorry," Tom said to Fergie when they discussed the order. "That was always Bax's way and generally he came out best."

"It makes some sense," Fergie agreed, "even if it is murder hoofing it up them trails. I must have walked three or four miles this afternoon and whoo-eee, did them water sacks get heavy on the way down!"

"Just be glad you ain't a foot soldier. See? There's something else to be happy about!"

They spent the better part of four days making their way through the sierra. There were only two rough spots, one a sharp-walled gully which required considerable work with picks and shovels before they could ease the wagons down the slope and up the other side, desperately hanging onto ropes or tugging at them all the while. The second obstacle was a pile of fallen rock which could not be avoided. Again the picks and shovels came out, and by pulling some rocks out of the way and tamping dirt into crevices between others they managed to build enough of a road to get the wagons across without wrecking them.

"If I could be sure that there were going to be much more of this, I believe I would be in favor of burning the wagons now and using the mules the rest of the way," Rawley said as they labored to get across the pile of rocks. "The wagons are useful but their price might become too high very soon!"

Fergie noticed that Rawley did not escape his share of

the hard, dirty work. He walked up to as many *tinajas* as anyone else and brought back as many containers of water; he set the example when it came to road building and swung a pick or shovel with as much effort as anyone else. Tom grinned skeptically when he mentioned Rawley's readiness to work.

"He knows that," he said. "And he knows that some of this gang wouldn't wait long to start complaining if he stood back and let the rest of us do it. He's a shrewd one, Bax is!"

Finally Hilario stood on a broad, open expanse of plain and pointed toward the south. The town of Cuatrocienegas lay several days' journey in that direction, he said; he was not sure of the distance but he had heard others say that a town of that name was to be found there. The going was easy, he thought, and he made it clear that he believed he had given them the guide service they had asked for.

Rawley thanked him and handed over the ten silver dollars, adding a small sack into which he put a measure of jerky and pinole. He gave Hilario a water bottle and one of the percussion pistols, along with powder, caps and balls, which they had taken from the *bandidos;* Hilario positively glowed with delight at the bonus. Rawley set the caravan on its way and accompanied Hilario a couple of miles back down the pass they had negotiated, then reclaimed the horse he had been riding and led the animal back to the remuda, where Paco and Fergie took charge.

"You know, I was wondering if maybe he wasn't just going to shoot Hilario," Fergie said to his uncle when they met later. "Just to save his ten dollars, I mean."

"Aw, that'd be way out of line," Tom protested, genuinely surprised at his nephew's skepticism. "Bax, he's a bastard, well enough, but he ain't that kind. He'll do what he says and he promised the money. But you notice he rode back part way with Hilario? I reckon he didn't trust the rest of us that much; I bet he wanted to make sure somebody didn't sneak off and get hisself ten easy dollars. That Mando there, him or Red either one, I wouldn't put it past them to try something like that."

"I sure ain't letting them know that *I* got any loose money," Fergie said.

"We'll get down fairly close to Cuatrocienegas and see what the situation looks like from there," Rawley told them the first night after Hilario had left them. If my maps are anywhere close to accurate, the town ought to be about two hundred miles from Parral. If there aren't any great obstacles between here and there, we ought to have this job finished within two weeks!"

CHAPTER FOURTEEN

Fergie would later think back to that evening beside the small fire built out of twigs and dried cholla branches, the only fuel they could find, and of the elation he had felt at hearing Rawley's comforting words. The memory would bring a wry grin to his cracked, wind-chapped lips, and he reminded himself never again to take an optimistic report at face value.

The day began promisingly enough. They had moved due south across the broad plain, aiming for a low mass of hills on the southern horizon. The wagons rolled easily across the flat, graveled terrain and they made excellent time. By midday, however, they could all see that the mass of hills was farther away than they had first thought and it was obvious that another chain of near-mountains lay across their path.

They came upon a trail of sorts in early afternoon, a fairly well-defined track leading down from the mountains, and Rawley set them upon it. As they moved closer to the mountains, which grew more forbidding with every mile, they saw that they were actually a series of massive crests, very much like the range through which Hilario had led them. The trail ducked to the left behind the first crest, they saw, and seemed to be slanting upward.

"Hell, this ain't so much to be worrying about!" Paco grunted to Fergie when they had pointed the remuda into the opening.

The trail became steeper but it remained easy going as it wound up a broad plain lying between two of the big ridges. They were well into the maze of crests and valleys when they made camp that night, and the men began laying bets on when they would see the town and who would catch the first glimpse of it.

Tom, who took the point the next morning, rode back an hour after they had gotten under way and reported possible trouble ahead. The trail they were following, he said, led down into a narrow, steep-walled canyon, creating a perfect spot for an ambush. They would not be able to post outriders at any distance from the wagons and thus they would be massed together and far more vulnerable to attack.

"Have you seen anything moving?" Rawley asked him.

"No, but there's something about the place that spooks me. It just don't feel the way it ought to. There ain't nothing I could put a finger on but still . . . it just don't feel right."

"Very well, that's good enough for me. Biscuit, ride back and tell Paco to bring the horses up nearer the wagons. Corto, Frenchy, Tom, let's move up and inspect the situation more closely."

They found that the canyon was indeed ideal for an ambush. The track led through the floor of the canyon, cutting through almost vertical walls that rose up a hundred feet in places. Portions of the canyon wall had broken off, leaving enormous piles of rock in places that squeezed the passageway into a corridor no more than fifty feet wide.

"There would be plenty of places to hide in there," Rawley said after he had snapped open a telescope and glassed the area briefly.

"Anybody in there, they'd sure find it hard to miss when we rode by," Tom commented.

"Hmmmm. Not very promising," Rawley mused when he had completed his more thorough search. "An ideal spot for the kind of mischief we do not need. And I see no other way of getting around it, either."

Mountains blocked either side of the canyon; from all appearances they would have to go far out of their way to detour the spot, even assuming that another passage could be found. Rawley scanned the surrounding area and shrugged as he snapped the telescope together and replaced it in its little leather case.

"There might be a crossing out there," he said, looking off to the mountains on either side of the canyon, "but how long would it take to find it?"

"There's one way we could stiffen up the odds a little," Frenchy suggested. "We could put a man with a rifle up there on the wall of that canyon. And another one over there on that other side. If they was good shots and knew their business, they could sure make things pretty warm for anybody down there in them rocks."

"Of course anyone up there might be an easy mark for them if they decided to rush him," Rawley pointed out. "But with men on both sides they ought to be able to protect each other fairly well. No, wait: I see a spot over there that ought to do; that's a thirty-foot straight cut beneath that shelf there. A man on top of that would be very hard to get at!"

"Me and Frenchy could handle that," Tom offered. "I reckon we're still the best hands with a rifle in the outfit, huh?"

"Be sure you carry some extra tubes for those rifles," Rawley said. "You won't have much time to reload, so go up there prepared for a lot of quick firing."

Tom and Frenchy sat down beside one of the wagons and began stuffing cartridges into the copper tubes holding the Spencers' loads, seven rounds to a tube; they carried five extra tubes, allowing them to get off over forty shots in a matter of a very few minutes.

"We'll send one wagon through at a time, and the rest of you can help from one end or the other," Rawley told his men when he had outlined the situation for them. "We might as well get to it right away; it won't be any easier later on if they're waiting for us."

"If who's waiting for us?" Red, the surly teamster, demanded. "And how many? What are they? Indians? More of them Mexicans?"

"We don't know that," Rawley repeated, giving the man a sour look. "But the situation looks very unpromising and—"

"Godamighty, we're farting around like the world was coming to an end and you don't even know nothing for sure! If that don't beat all!"

"As I said, the situation looks very unpromising and Tom has a definite feeling about it being a bad one," Rawley said. His voice had become very soft but it had a definitely dangerous edge. "That happens to be quite enough for me; if you're not convinced you are perfectly welcome to go through on your own. But you'll do it soon, one way or the other, if you don't want my knife in your throat!"

Red suddenly blanched and looked down at the ground. Fergie saw the man's Adam's apple bobbing up and down as he swallowed furiously.

"Aw, I was just funning around," he mumbled. "It didn't mean nothing."

"It very nearly meant too much for you," Rawley warned. "Now, if that is settled, here is the way I propose to handle the situation."

He repeated that they would take only one wagon through the canyon at a time; there was too much danger of the mules and wagons getting entangled in a pileup if they all went together and one team were to be killed in their traces. As nearly as anyone could tell, the defile broadened into a small valley about six hundred yards ahead; that area would serve as a good spot for regrouping, since it looked to be well away from any rocks that might hide an attacker. Tom and Frenchy would be on the cliffs above to give supporting fire if it were needed. Biscuit was to stay with the wagons until the last one had gone through and would follow it; Rawley and Corto were to go with the first wagon and wait at the regrouping area. Paco and Fergie were told to take the horses through last of all.

"If it starts popping don't you bother stopping to shoot back at anything," Tom said to his nephew as they made their final arrangements. "The best way to stay alive is to get low on your horse, stay there and ride like hell!"

"I'll do it," Fergie promised, nervous and already trembling with excitement. "Good luck, Uncle Tom!"

"And the same to you, Fergie. Get after it now and don't never look back. Remember, them that stops is most likely to stay stopped—for good!"

With that he hefted his rifle and the extra cartridge tubes and started scrambling up to the vantage point Rawley had spotted. Frenchy went up the opposite side, and as soon as they had settled into place they waved the go-ahead signal.

Rawley and Corto moved their horses into place in front of the first wagon, which was being driven by Becker, a stolid Dutchman who had uttered no more than a dozen words, possibly, since joining the crew. Becker had shoved a stubby-barreled shotgun into a boot he had attached to the front of the wagon bed near his right knee; he checked the loads in the wicked-looking weapon—Paco claimed that it was loaded with bits of horseshoe nails—and nodded his readiness.

They eased down into the canyon at a walk. Rawley quickened the pace to a trot as soon as the grade had leveled out; he also motioned for Corto to take up a position behind the wagon. They passed through the cut without incident. As soon as they had reached the spot selected for regrouping Becker halted his team, wrapped the reins around the brake and moved to the back of his wagon to face the path over which he had just traveled. He hefted a Spencer and waited. Rawley lifted his right hand and waved the next wagon through.

Red, who happened to be the second teamster in line, snapped the reins and clucked at his mules. He walked them down the slope and then slapped them into a brisk trot. He had gone about two hundred yards when Frenchy whistled shrilly and fired a shot into a pile of rocks at Red's left.

"Yeee-hawwwww!" Red yelled, slapping the reins again and cursing the mules into a gallop. "Get up there, you devils, or I'll roast you myself!"

A scream had punctuated the blast of Frenchy's rifle, a sound of such pure agony that Fergie could not believe it had come from a human throat. A figure rose up out of the rocks into which Frenchy had fired, toppling out of them and limply tumbling down until hitting a jagged outcropping below. Fergie looked again and saw a human form resting on the rocks: the man wore an Indian-style shirt, a long, dirty garment that came almost to his knees and was cinched about his waist with a leather belt holding a knife scabbard.

Frenchy's shot gave the signal for an outburst of whooping that sent a shiver of animal terror racing up and down Fergie's stiff back. He had heard whoops like that before, long ago when a small party of Comanche raiders had briefly attacked the Harrison ranch house; they quickly saw that the ranch's defenders had an impregnable position and had given up the attack after peppering the house with a few arrows. The sound of their shrill, yipping cries, something like a coyote's lonesome call but far more threatening, still remained vividly clear in the youth's mind.

Tom and Frenchy both began firing down into the canyon as Red urged his team to an even faster pace. Rawley, Corto and Becker also began firing, though at a slower rate. Fergie stood up in his stirrups to dart quick looks down at the canyon, but, except for the man Frenchy had shot to initiate the action, he saw not a single trace of an enemy. The horses and mules threw up their heads and stamped nervously at the screeching and firing that issued from the canyon, but he and Paco managed to hold them in a compact bunch.

Mando, the next teamster in line, drove his wagon down into the defile as soon as Red had covered half the distance to Becker's wagon. Pilón and Cruz followed suit. Arrows whizzed across the trail; two mules were struck but neither had been hit badly enough to be slowed at once. Rawley found himself a ledge at the far end of the canyon and scrambled up onto it with as much speed as he could manage. The added height gave him a better view and he began firing more rapidly.

"Get going!" Tom yelled down, motioning to Paco and

Fergie when Cruz, driving the last wagon, had gotten nearly across the open space. "Move out!"

Paco pointed the lead animals into the defile and whipped them down the grade. Fergie herded the stragglers along and then bent low, getting as far down onto his horse's neck as he could and hefting the big Colt in his right hand. His palm was sweating so profusely he nearly dropped the weapon after getting it out of the saddle holster. He remembered Biscuit's lesson, how the man had plastered himself against his horse's mane, and he tried to do exactly the same thing. He caught a glimpse of a dirty white shirt off to his right as his horse hit the level portion of the canyon and lined into a full gallop; he snapped off a quick shot but could not have said whether the bullet came anywhere near the mark. Once he had gotten well under way, he became enveloped in the dust cloud raised by the herd of horses and could see no farther than his horse's head.

They came out of the skirmish with only one casualty. Cruz, the man who had introduced Fergie to chicken roasted inside a mud shell, took an arrow in his chest when he was two-thirds of the way across the canyon. He had held onto the reins until the mules pulled up beside the other wagons, but by that time his mouth was rimmed with a pink froth and his eyes could not focus.

The canyon opened out into a broad plain leading away from the line of mountains. Fergie and Paco spent nearly an hour chasing down stray animals; by the time they had the remuda collected and under control the men were ready to move again.

"Cruz took an arrow through the lungs and kicked off," Tom told them as he came out to the herd with Corto. "We've got to cut out a couple more mules—some of them look more like pincushions than mules by now; Mando's killing them to put them out of their misery. Otherwise we come out of it in pretty good shape, it looks like."

Fergie blinked and swallowed hard at hearing the news about Cruz. He had grown to like the little man, who had a sly, engaging air and told scandalously exaggerated stories about his successes with women. Or at least Fergie had suspected that they were exaggerated; he could not imagine any woman losing a moment's peace of mind over that bent figure and scarred face.

Paco whistled the youth to attention and pointed to a pair of horses getting away from the main body of the herd. He spurred after them, leaving Paco and Tom with the chore of cutting out the mules they wanted. For the remainder of the day he had his hands full: the battle had spooked the horses and it took a long time for the herd to settle down.

That evening, as he walked to the wagons after finishing his chores with the remuda, he noticed a pair of men well off to one side. They were wielding shovels and, when he saw a blanket-covered form beside them, he concluded that they were burying Cruz. Walking over to them, he offered his help, and Mando, one of the men, threw him his shovel with a grin of thanks.

No one else stood by as they finished digging the hole and lowered the stiff corpse into it, then shoveled back the dirt and patted it down firmly. When they walked back to the wagons and stowed their shovels away the rest of the men were busily eating and paid no attention to them. Fergie had tried to think of something appropriate to say as he and Becker, the other gravedigger, had stood beside the open grave, but he could not remember anything which sounded suitable. He remembered the funerals of his parents but could not dredge up any of the words used at those services; mostly he remembered a sort of mental numbness, that and the wavering strains of a hymn they had sung. He could remember the hymn's tune but not one of the words.

"What kind of Indians was them?" Fergie asked his uncle later that evening. "I swear, I didn't get but barely a peek at any of them."

"Lipan Apaches, most likely. It was hard to tell from where I was standing, and I for damned sure wasn't going to get close enough to ask. You can be mighty glad you didn't get a better look either—it just might have been your last one!"

"How many of them was there?"

"Fifteen, maybe twenty at the outside. Or maybe I seen the same ones more than once. They was hopping around right smartly there for a while, jumping in and out of them rocks and all."

"You didn't get a good look at them either? I thought sure somebody'd be able to see them good. I got a shot off at one when I was chasing them horses down through there but I don't know if I came anywheres close to him or not."

"That's about the way it goes," Tom told him. "Most of the time I was just shooting to make them keep their heads down. Frenchy, he was pretty lucky, getting him a clear shot at that one the way he did."

"Did . . . did you shoot any of them?"

"I think I might have winged one or two. We was just mighty lucky that they didn't have themselves a repeater apiece, else there'd have been more of us laying out there, I can tell you that for sure. I think most of them just had bows and arrows. There was a few old muskets in that crowd, I think, but not enough to make any real difference."

"Well, young man, what did you think of your first running gun battle?" Rawley asked, approaching them with a cup of coffee in his hand. "Would you rather fight Indians or *bandidos*?"

"Neither one, not if I've got any choice about it," Fergie answered. "There didn't seem to be that much to either one of them fights, you know? I mean, there was a lot of banging and yelling but . . . oh, I don't know, it just wasn't like anything I'd ever have expected. Course, I can see that it was serious business, what with Cruz getting killed and all, but . . ."

"It wasn't so very different from most of the actions I've seen," Rawley said, "and I believe Tom would agree with me there. All in all we came out surprisingly well, I believe. We seem to have done more harm than was done to us, which is always an advantage, and we can continue on to finish our work."

Fergie ended his part of the conversation by going out to stand his turn of guard duty. He could still remember with hair-raising clarity the din of the battle in the canyon, the yelling and the banging of rifles; a sick, nauseous feeling permeated his midsection when he thought of the dead Cruz. They had lain side by side during the earlier battle, firing from under the same wagon, and now Cruz lay in a hole in a godforsaken part of Mexico. He had seen three people killed, counting the child back in the village, since crossing the Rio Grande, and as far as he could determine each of the deaths could have been avoided by the use of a little common sense, or maybe by the saving presence of a little humanity or luck. Not one of the deaths had anything heroic or noble about it, so far as he could tell.

They saw no further signs of the Indians, which suited most of them perfectly. Once out of the canyon they had an easy downhill pull, and the mountains gradually slipped away as they drove out onto a vast, empty plain. The trail they had been following melted away quickly but there was no need for it; they could have taken almost any route they wanted so long as it was in a direction other than north. A few rock-encrusted hills jutted up out of the plain, but the wagons could easily circle any of them.

The scrape with the Indians at first had the effect of relieving some of the tensions which had been built up during the trek. Then, paradoxically, it seemed to inflame them to an even higher degree. That morning, as Fergie strode away from the wagons, still angry with his uncle, they burst into open flame.

Red, the loud-voiced and arrogant teamster, had been extremely forward in proclaiming his contempt for the land into which they were traveling, as well as its inhabitants. The *bandidos* had been a cowardly, inept lot, he frequently announced, and the Indians had simply been too stupid to mount a successful ambush.

"Hell, you could get you three or four good old Texas

boys," he brayed that morning, "and come down here and take over the whole damned country! I bet we could all be kings of Mexico if we put our heads to it and spent a month or six weeks going to work on these worthless people down here!"

"That other three or four would have to be a lot smarter than you," Mando told him, looking up with obvious distaste. "And you, you fat slob, you couldn't be king of a pig-pen!"

"Why, you filthy little greaser! I'll stomp your head for that!"

He advanced toward Mando and the others fell backward in their eagerness to get out of the way. Red was a big man, well over two hundred pounds in weight, and had a pair of powerful-looking arms. No one had been eager to tangle with him, though no one liked his loud, overbearing manner.

Mando gave away a good four inches in height to the man and perhaps thirty or forty pounds. His weight had been compacted into his shoulders and forearms by years of hard work, however, and he looked to be almost as powerful as anyone in the entire crew.

Instead of meeting Red's charge head to head, as the onlookers expected, Mando fell off to one side and kicked out with his left foot as Red neared him. Every man in the group heard a distinct snap as his heavy oxhide boot thudded into Red's leg, striking him just below the knee. Red bellowed angrily and fell over. Gritting out an oath, he clawed at his hip, drew his pistol and fired.

Mando pitched backward, clutching his stomach. Almost immediately the front of his shirt turned dark and blood began seeping down over his fingers as he held his hands to the wound. A shocked, unbelieving expression spread over his face; it was quickly followed by a blank, unseeing look and his hands fell away from the wound.

"By God, he got him plumb dead center!" Frenchy exclaimed.

"Right smack-dab in the middle," Biscuit muttered. "He's done for, bound to be, with a hit like that!"

"What's going on here?" Rawley shouted, running toward the men. "Who fired that shot?"

When he saw what had happened—no one needed to give him the details—his lips tightened into a narrow slit. Tom, who happened to be standing near him, swore later that his eyes flamed up almost as though tiny but very powerful fires were burning inside his skull.

"You fool!" he grated, looking down at Red. "Two wagons out of commission now, thanks to your incredible stupidity and that big mouth of yours!"

"Aw, he was just a Mexican," Red grumbled. "One of the other boys can drive his rig. I'll be all set to drive just as soon as I can get this leg of mine tended to."

"And now we're two men short!" Rawley said, paying no attention to Red's words. "And at a time when we were already shorthanded! Of all the idiotic acts!"

Suddenly his hand darted into his coat, emerging with the small, .36-caliber Colt he carried under his left armpit. Red's eyes widened when he saw the pistol appear in his hand; before he could cry out or get his own pistol aimed, Rawley fired. A small, dark hole appeared in the very center of Red's forehead. He sank back upon the gravel, seeming almost to melt into the ground.

"Godamighty, did you see that!"

"Where'd he get that gun?"

"Let this be a lesson to all of you," Rawley said, ignoring their awed comments as he ejected the spent shell from his pistol and inserted another round into the smoking chamber. "We have no men to spare; you will have to wait until we complete our journey to settle whatever differences you may have with each other. Anyone who disables one of my men will die, whoever he is, and you may depend on that!"

With that he bent over Red and unfastened the man's gunbelt, taking the pistol from the ground where it had fallen; he threw them both into the back of the nearest wagon. He also removed Mando's knife from the man's belt—he had not carried a pistol—and threw that into the wagon too. He waited a moment and then lashed the men into activity with a few harsh words. Two men dragged shovels from a wagon and fell to work at digging shallow graves. Others began harnessing mules and hitching them to their wagons.

"Go get Fergie from the horse herd," Rawley said to Corto. "Biscuit, you and the kid will have to handle their wagons, at least for the time being. We'll see if we can't pick up some extra men in that next town."

CHAPTER FIFTEEN

Fergie had driven wagons and buggies enough to be able to handle the big freight rig, though he would not have wanted to try taking it through some of the rough country they had passed. Having only two mules to contend with and a light load in the box made the wagon easier to control, he found. Biscuit showed him how to fit and adjust the heavy set of harness and assured him that he would be able to handle the mules.

"All you need to do is get a little uglier to look at and learn yourself some fancier cusswords," the man said. "Time you do that and start smelling a little more like one of them lop-eared jennies, you'll be a fine teamster!"

"And to think that I had to go through all this just to end up sitting on a wagon box looking at the back end of a pair of mules!"

"That's a right inspiring sight," Biscuit said, acting very solemn. "And it must be a right powerful one, too. Did you ever see a teamster that didn't know the answer to everything under the sun?"

There were no more mountains in their way, a fact for which they were all grateful. Tom led them south and they made excellent time, winding around an occasional hill but always keeping to level, easy terrain. As Fergie was completing his second day on the wagon box, Tom rode back from the point to report the presence of a town ahead.

"Looks like it might could hold five hundred or a thousand people," he said to Rawley. "I could see a church and a square, I think it was. And some greenery too—so maybe it'll live up to its name."

"Oh? How so?"

"The way I figure it, that can't be no place but Cuatro-cienegas. And a '*cienega*,' that's a well, or maybe a spring or even just a swampy place. Anyhow, it means a wet spot."

"Then let us indeed hope that it lives up to its name," Rawley agreed. "We could all benefit from a bath and some laundry facilities. Suppose you go on ahead and give the place an examination."

"We might could use a little extra time to grease up them hubs and get ourselves squared around," Tom suggested. "It might do us all good if we could loosen up a little."

"Yes, and we'll also look for some replacements," Rawley added. "We'll need another teamster or two, especially if the way ahead is bad. I'm tempted to try getting across with the men we have now; they could each split up the extra money, which might ease the situation somewhat for them."

"That'd be a little risky. Everybody doing double guard duty, cutting down on the patrols, it's a good way to get into trouble."

"Exactly," Rawley agreed. "And the main thing is to get across this next portion safely. Well, we'll see about all that tomorrow if the town looks hospitable enough to warrant a visit."

Excitement spread through the camp that evening, following closely on the heels of the news about the nearby town. Rawley called the men together and announced his intentions. If the town appeared to be safe, he promised, they would spend two days resting and making the repairs needed for the last leg of their journey. They would take turns visiting the town, half on one day and half on the other, if the situation allowed it, and he would make an attempt to recruit additional teamsters. His men obviously cared much more about visiting the town than about replenishing their ranks, and he had to caution them again that they would avoid the town if it harbored a military detachment.

Rawley nodded approvingly when Tom reported, later in the day, that there was no sign of a military force in the town. He presided over the drawing of lots early the next morning, making his own selection last, and awarded a short straw to both Fergie and Tom, meaning that they had to stay in camp and work during the first day of rest. Before taking off for the day of revelry in the town, however, they moved the wagons up to a campsite about a half mile from the outskirts of Cuatrocienegas, camping beside a ditch carrying water out to the fields.

"It's just as well we're staying here today," Tom said as he and Fergie began checking the wagons for flaws. "Them other boys can get the town oiled up good and running smooth; we'll be able to get the best of it tomorrow."

Apart from a few dry hubs the wagons proved to need little in the way of repairs. They were stoutly made, and Rawley's care in selecting the easiest routes meant that they had been subjected to minimum stresses during the trip.

"You take care of your gear and it'll take care of you," Tom said as they packed grease into a hub. "That's an old army rule and it makes a lot of sense, I always thought."

The villagers' enterprise ensured that those men left at the wagons did not miss a great deal. Toward noon of that first day, Rawley looked up to see a group of people advancing toward them. Several women could be seen, along with a burro carrying a precariously balanced load. Upon coming closer to the camp, one of the men stepped forward and offered to supply them all with a hot meal, pulque and tequila for a nominal sum.

"And I was wondering if they were planning an attack!" Rawley exclaimed when he had learned the true purpose of their mission.

"They might have that in the back of their mind," Tom advised. "It wouldn't hurt none if we let them see that we're all armed."

The villagers began unloading bottles, baskets, pots and sheets of tin from the burro. The pots contained beans, already cooked, and the tins were to be used for cooking tortillas, which some of the women began patting out. Sacks of charcoal appeared and soon the smell of hot food, the first Fergie had experienced since leaving San Antonio, spread over the campground. The women had laced the beans with chiles and hunks of goat meat, making a rich, tangy mixture, and Fergie ate until he groaned. Bottles of mescal, tequila and pulque appeared, but Rawley chased the vendors off before anyone could become obstreperously drunk. By pulling the wagons into a big, pentagonal figure and connecting ropes across the open spaces, they made a rude corral for the horses and thus dispensed with the need for one of the two guards usually posted at their camps.

No one came near the camp that night, not even the men who had gone into town. Rawley grunted knowingly the next morning when he counted heads and found that half his crew was still in Cuatrocienegas. He consulted every man left in the camp, seeking his opinion on what equipment they needed from the town, and wrote down the items named, mostly leather goods to replace bits of worn-out harness.

"We'll have to chase the others out and get them back to work," he said to Tom, Biscuit and Fergie. "That is, if they can stand up!"

"After that, it'll be off to an *acequia* for us," Tom said, nudging Fergie, "and trying to scrape some of this dirt off. Look in our warbag, will you, and see if you can't find us that hunk of soap, huh?"

"Aww, a bath?" Fergie groaned.

"Sure enough. Didn't you notice how all them women stayed upwind of us when they was cooking yesterday? And you could tell by looking that they was a pretty rank bunch theirselves, so you can just bet we're a mite woolly around the edges. Besides, it might make you feel good."

"A dirty soldier always attracts lice and vermin," Rawley added. "Eventually they will have their revenge; most often people like that are the first to fall to a disease."

"All right, if you're going to make a case out of it I'll find the blasted soap," Fergie conceded.

He searched through their belongings and brought out a fresh shirt and another pair of trousers, along with a clean pair of socks, then found the cube of yellow laundry soap they had carried from their ranch house on the Nueces. Tom got himself out a change of clothing and tied the bundle behind his saddle. Rawley led them into the town and they began searching for the missing members of the crew. Most of them had gone home with the women who hung around the cantina at night, and within an hour Rawley had them all mounted and moving out to camp. Loud groans and protests were the order of the day, especially when Rawley made it clear that he expected them to finish the work begun by the portion of the crew who had drawn short straws, but they fell to work and gradually recovered from the effects of their debauch.

Tom led his nephew down to the *acequia* which carried water from the wells to the fields outside the town. A few people were at work between the rows of corn but otherwise the two had the area to themselves. Fergie had to laugh when he saw his uncle stripped naked; his body retained its natural shade of white but it contrasted ludicrously with his dark hands and face.

"You look about the same," Tom said when he learned the source of Fergie's amusement. "But we'll both be a couple or three shades lighter all over when we get finished here, so hurry up with that soap."

They took their time about it but when they walked out of the *acequia* they were both somewhat paler than when they had entered it. They sat on the grassy bank until the sun had baked the water off their skins, then put on their change of clothing, rolled the discarded items into a bundle and rode back into town. Tom stopped along the way to bargain with a housewife; she agreed to wash and dry their clothes as well as mend the most obvious rents in return for a peso.

They stopped first at the cantina and ordered food, choosing generous amounts of almost everything to be found in the kitchen. After gorging almost to the point of stupefaction they walked out into the square. Rawley beckoned to them from across the open plaza and they went over to join him.

"I have found only one man who seems to know anything about driving mules," he told them. "But he claims that he has moved freight from Monterrey to both Parral and Chihuahua and, according to Corto, he seems to know the difference between a hame and a trace. Your bartender's relative knew nothing about any of it, I might add."

"I wasn't vouching for him," Tom replied. "Well, one's better than none in a case like this. We could angle off to the south and pick up that road from Monterrey; it ought not to be no more than three days south of here, I guess."

"That's just what this old fellow advises," Rawley said. "Apparently it is out of the question to try going due west of here; the water problem becomes acute in that direction."

"I'd always heard it was a mighty dry stretch between here and there," Tom agreed. "And it'd be a real help if that man's really been that way before."

Tom and Fergie spent the remainder of the day relaxing in the town. The cantina's women began appearing after noon; without exception they were a bleary-eyed lot and showed the effects of the previous night's carousing. Tom smiled courteously but shook his head when the first two approached him.

They ate three complete meals during the twelve hours they stayed in Cuatrocienegas. The scent of cooking beans, along with the characteristic odor of cooking tortillas, served to excite their hunger immeasurably. The owner of the cantina topped off the feasting by laying huge slabs of barbecued goat in front of them. Fergie mixed the pungent red sauce, glistening with globules of fat, into the beans on his plate, stirred in a helping of rice and gathered it all up with a tortilla.

"That's the nice thing about pinole and jerky," Tom said when his nephew belched mightily during the ride out to the camp that night. "It sure does make you appreciate good cooking!"

"It don't even have to be very good for you to appreciate it," Fergie replied. "I've eaten better but it sure wasn't bad!"

They left Cuatrocienegas the next morning as soon as they could get the crew together. Belisario, the teamster Rawley had located, turned out to be a very old man with snow-white hair and a surprisingly spry manner. He scuttled around the mules as he harnessed them, muttering to them in a garbled, incoherent Spanish as he adjusted the hames and checked the bridles, then leaped up onto the wagon box and sat there like a monarch until Rawley gave the signal for them to move out.

Belisario—most of the men soon shortened his name to Beeley, which he did not appear to mind—had agreed that they would do best to head southwest until they crossed the Monterrey-Chihuahua trail, then follow it. The more direct line, going straight across from Cuatrocienegas, was no good, he said.

"*Es una jornada del muerto*," he growled, shaking his head vehemently.

"He means it's a killer," Tom explained to Rawley. "It might or it might not be; no way of telling."

"I tend to vote with the old man," Rawley decided. "After all, if it were a trail that had much traffic, then that town would have showed some sign of it, don't you think? I rather doubt that too many people have gone that way."

"It makes sense to me," Tom agreed. "It seems to me I remember hearing stories from back in '49 and '50, when we first come to Texas, about people making it from Monterrey to Chihuahua on their way to the gold fields in California. There was a right smart of them went that way, so I heard, so maybe there's something to it after all."

"Besides, the old feller's been over that other way," Biscuit added, overhearing their talk. "Or he claims he has; it might be best to stick to what he knows something about."

The journey soon became boring, or so Fergie found it. He alternated with Biscuit in driving the fifth wagon, which broke up the monotony to some extent, but even so the trip began to seem as though it would never end. The land leveled off into a gray and tan blanket spreading for miles in every direction. A faint purple line against the northern and southern horizons suggested the presence of far-off mountains. The days rolled on, each like the one before it, and they seemed to be making no progress at all across that dry sea.

They took the better part of three days to link up with the

Monterrey-Chihuahua road, which proved to be only a very faint track lining out to the west, and they stayed on it for four days. At the end of that time they could make out another low, purple line to the west. Fergie felt a surge of emotion spreading out from his chest, but he later learned that the rise he saw marked a false beginning for the Sierra Madres. Even so, he felt a warm elation every morning when he looked up at the distant mountains, which sheltered the site of the fabled Copper Canyon as well as the locations for a hundred stirring tales of mines and treasure.

Rawley began consulting his map several times each day; he also held numerous conferences with Beeley and attempted to describe to him some of the principal landmarks they were to use for homing in on the rendezvous. They had approached the few villages along the way with caution, checking each of them for the presence of troops, and had avoided the larger towns, such as Parras, altogether; consequently they had only a vague idea of their true location. Corto solved the impasse by riding in one afternoon and reporting that he had met a small party of vaqueros, one of whom knew the location of Don Esteban Plata's hacienda San Elizario, their target.

"It's about two days to the southwest, he told me," Corto said to Rawley. "If we aim to pass just north of that sugarloaf there and then keep angling southwest, we ought to run into it for sure, he claims."

"Excellent!" Rawley beamed.

They changed their line of march accordingly and a new spirit swept through the men. They were all extremely tired of herding the wagons along; the prospect of nearing the end of their journey made them all more alert. Rawley ordered his outriders to patrol even more carefully than ever; no one had heard any reports of troops or *bandidos* being in the area, but he was not a man to take any unnecessary chances. He also ordered Tom to scout ahead as far as he wished, holding back only for considerations of safety.

"I suspect that the French or their sympathizers might be watching the place," he explained. "After all, the owner's political sympathies should be fairly well known by this time. And even if the French are miles away we should still be cautious—they might want to help themselves to the rifles and forgo the pleasure of paying us for them!"

"I reckon you've got some ideas on how to keep that from happening," Tom observed.

"A few, but nothing specific yet; that will have to wait until we know more about the situation. But you may be sure that we will not be caught sleeping!"

Rawley adopted a different tactic once they had driven into what they considered to be the vicinity of the hacienda San Elizario. He sent out Frenchy, ordering him to remain halfway between Tom and the wagons and to ride back at once if either of them saw the hacienda or riders. When both men came in that evening to report having seen nothing, Rawley announced that they would go into a more permanent camp the next day.

"We cannot afford to have all these rifles wandering about the countryside," he said. "Tomorrow we must find a suitable canyon and put the wagons out of sight. As soon as we make contact . . . well, we'll have to see about that when the time comes."

CHAPTER SIXTEEN

The country into which they had been driving became rougher with every mile as they neared the sierra; they had no trouble in finding a thickly wooded canyon which would give the wagons adequate protection. The trees, a mixture of juniper and a kind of oak which Fergie had never seen before, fronted on a broad, grassy meadow that would provide ample grazing for the remuda.

Rawley posted men at various points overlooking approaches to the canyon and arranged a schedule to ensure that no one had to man a guard post for more than half a day. He took Corto with him and rode out to the southeast, leaving Tom to try investigating the area to the southwest of the wagons.

"If you find the hacienda, mention that you were sent by Ramon Vásquez," Rawley told him. "He was the agent I dealt with in the United States and his name ought to get you to Don Esteban. Have them arrange to meet us just north of that flat-topped mountain there to the south. They should be there at, say, noon tomorrow. We can make the final negotiations there."

They rode off in their separate directions. Rawley met a party of vaqueros three hours later who directed him and Corto to the hacienda. He found that the establishment looked even more impressive than he had expected; an adobe wall enclosed the principal buildings and, being whitewashed, sat upon the broad, grassy plain like a huge, snow-white barge.

Upon riding through the archway—there was no gate; a battered, wooden-wheeled wagon standing beside it suggested that it might be used to barricade the ten-foot-wide opening in time of siege—he saw that the buildings were less impressive when viewed at close range. The buildings still had a pleasing proportion, managing to look solid without giving the effect of being ponderous, but the details marred the overall effect. The walls enclosed a massive rectangle, an open space measuring perhaps one hundred by fifty feet, and rooms had been built against three sides of the outer wall. Riding closer, Rawley saw that the fourth wall, the one farthest from his approach, extended only partway down the fourth side; the remainder of the rectangle was given over to corrals, which stretched a considerable distance away from the central structure. He passed close to one range of rooms and saw that the doorjambs were rotting away and that many of them had no doors at all, though he caught glimpses of women and children inside them; in other cases he noticed that the windowsills and doors—in fact, every piece of wood used in the construction—were either rotting or badly cracked by the elements. None of the woodwork looked as though it had ever been painted. A flock of children, all wearing a shirt-like garment that could equally well have been a dress, played along one side of the dusty square. They grew silent and fell back as Rawley and Corto rode toward them.

"*Buscamos Don Esteban Plata,*" Corto said to a squat, scowling man who came toward them.

They were told that Don Esteban was dead; his eldest son, Don Eduardo, now ruled over the hacienda.

"Ask him if Don Eduardo is here," Rawley directed.

They were told that he was at home and were asked the nature of their business. Rawley hesitated for only a moment; he had already prepared an innocuous story in case the situation did not appear exactly as he would have liked.

"Tell him that we met a friend of Don Esteban's in the United States," Rawley instructed Corto. "This man, Ramon Vásquez, recommended that we stop by the hacienda to pay our respects when we passed this way. We wish instead to offer our condolences to Don Eduardo."

The man invited them to get down from their horses. He called for a servant to take charge of their mounts and he directed them to some benches under a vine-covered *ramada* in one corner of the complex of buildings. Don Eduardo, he assured them, would be there shortly.

"My father died three months ago," Don Eduardo said after he had joined them and had welcomed them to his establishment. "Too soon, I regret to say, to witness the completion of the struggle in which we all believed. If you met Ramon Vásquez and he directed you this way, I need hardly inquire about your business."

He spoke reasonably good English, strongly accented but freely flowing. A man of about forty, he wore a pair of elegantly tailored moleskin trousers, a white shirt that was as sparkling as the walls of his hacienda, and a short jacket that barely touched the tops of his trousers. He clapped his hands to summon a servant and ordered drinks brought for all of them. Rawley, whom Tom had already instructed on the niceties of dealing with an upper-class Mexican landowner, expounded briefly on the charm of the hacienda. Don Eduardo smiled gracefully and apologized for the primitive nature of the reception he was offering; he attributed this to the French and their disruption of everyday life in Mexico.

"Have they been active in this region?" Rawley asked.

"Not at all; this is *Juarista* country," Don Eduardo said, pouring brandy which the servant had brought. "Your health, *señores!* Ahhh! No, we have not had any French troops in this region for some months. But farther to the south they have been active. Consequently we cannot get goods from that area. I presume that you are bringing us, er, some tools for remedying that deplorable situation?"

"I have five hundred Spencer repeaters, approximately, and about fifty rounds of ammunition per rifle," Rawley said. "Señor Vásquez made a tentative purchase in San Antonio; I have the papers here."

"Yes. Very good," Don Eduardo said, taking the envelope Rawley handed him and leafing through the pages it enclosed. "I am not familiar with this rifle. A r-r-re—what did you call it?"

"A repeater. With your permission I can show you how it works."

Don Eduardo sent another servant to bring the rifles from Rawley's and Corto's saddles. When they were produced, Rawley handed one to his host and used the other to demonstrate his points. He showed how to remove the tube from the stock, how to load it with seven cartridges and how to work them through the rifle's action. Don Eduardo had evidently never seen or heard of a repeating rifle and he was fascinated.

They walked to the archway and took up a position in front of the massive building. Rawley pointed to a small boulder standing fifty yards away, levered a round into the chamber and began firing. He got off six rounds in well under a minute, working the action so smoothly the booming reports rolled out one after the other in rapid succession. Chips flew off the rock with every shot, attesting to Rawley's marksmanship.

"Go ahead, try it yourself," Rawley suggested.

Don Eduardo emptied the rifle, working the action with difficulty at first but quickly growing accustomed to it.

"*Que bueno!*" he murmured as he ejected the last shell and hefted the rifle admiringly. "I would not have believed it possible!"

"Imagine what forty or fifty men with these could do to an old-fashioned infantry regiment advancing on your hacienda," Rawley told him. "These five hundred rifles will give you a great deal of power!"

"And you really have five hundred of these marvels?"

"We have about that many. We had to use some of them on the trip across from Texas but there won't be many less than that. Er, Vásquez mentioned that you would buy them for fifty dollars each."

"Yes, that is the sum he stated in his report. It is expensive but I believe the expense will be fully justified by the results. When can you make your delivery?"

"Probably within the next three or four days," Rawley said. "But that brings up the problem of how the exchange is to be accomplished. My men—well, you will understand that I had to recruit a group of extremely villainous rascals to ensure a safe delivery. I . . . I would hesitate to bring them very close to your hacienda; they might take it upon themselves to revert back to their former occupation. It would be safer for all of us if we were to meet somewhere else—a more open spot, well away from danger."

"I understand and agree. It is not for the hacienda's safety that I agree with you, you understand; we are reasonably well skilled at fighting. But it would be best to avoid every possible source of conflict, eh?"

"Let me scout around for a possible site while the rifles are arriving," Rawley suggested. "Perhaps one of your men could meet me at noon two days from now? I should have more definite information by that time, and we should be able to agree upon a mutually acceptable place and time for the exchange."

"That will be quite satisfactory," Don Eduardo agreed. "And in the interval I can begin preparations for assembling the payment."

After agreeing with Don Eduardo on the place for their next meeting, Rawley and Corto left the hacienda. They traveled due north and did not swing back to the west, and the canyon hiding the wagons, until they had assured themselves that they were not being followed. They arrived back in camp late that afternoon.

"He's a sly one," Rawley told them as they circled around the cooking fire for their meal. "He understood exactly what I meant when I said I wanted to make the exchange well away from his ranch house."

"It'd be a nice little windfall for him if he could get the rifles and keep the money too," Biscuit observed.

"In any case we must take every precaution," Rawley told them. "He might be a paragon of honesty but I don't want to take that for granted."

Tom and Rawley went out the next day to begin scouting for a site which they could use for delivering the rifles. They wanted a spot on a broad, open plain, one which would offer a minimum chance for being surprised and which would be well away from both the hacienda and their own campground.

"This looks pretty good right here," Tom said later that

morning as they rested their horses on a low ridge and looked off to the south. "We could hold the wagons back behind this ridge and move them out through that little cut yonder. You could put a man up on the shoulder of that peak there; he ought to be able to see everything for miles around."

"It will give them some protection too," Rawley noted. "They can advance across that plain there without fear of being ambushed. Yes, I believe this will do very well for the place."

"How about the wagons? You aiming to sell them to him too?"

"No, I think not. I doubt if he would have much use for them. We ought to be able to get a better price in Parral—a mining town ought to need wagons constantly. We can sell off most of the horses and mules there too, I should think. Then, my friend, we begin the best part of all! We should be rich men indeed by the end of the summer!"

"Just hope you ain't rich *dead* mean," Tom warned.

"Oh? Are you not going along with us?"

"I sort of doubt it. I feel sort of responsible for Fergie, and he . . . well, I just ain't sure but what an operation like that mightn't be a little too woolly for the likes of him."

"He's growing up, Tom; he's almost a man. You can't protect him forever, you know."

"I know that. But I reckon I ought to try, at least as long as I can."

"Perhaps something will happen to make you change your mind. I certainly hope so; the two of you should give us just the extra edge we need to make a guaranteed success of that venture."

Rawley and Tom met Don Eduardo's messenger the following day and gave him the location of the spot they had selected. The man nodded, saying that he knew the place well, and that Don Eduardo would be there with the money on the following day. Rawley then dispatched Corto to the site and instructed him to spend the night on the peak they had chosen for a lookout post. He was to hide his horse, first, and then to gather as large a pile of greasewood as he could. If he saw any sign that Don Eduardo was preparing a trap for them, he was to fire the pile and get away at once.

"He sure don't leave much to chance, does he?" Fergie muttered when he had heard Rawley's orders for the final disposition of his forces. "It'd be hard to run a sandy on *him!*"

"You're mighty right it would," Tom agreed. "And dangerous too! That's the nice part about riding with Bax—he sure does believe in protection."

"Even if other people have to suffer for it," Fergie said after a moment. "Like them people back there in that little village."

"Well, maybe that's part of it. It might be that you can't have the one without the other, did you ever think about it that way?"

"It ain't much of a thing to think about, is it?"

"I ain't so sure about that," Tom replied. "You might ought to do a whole lot of thinking about it, you being so keen on war and all that. And you might try, just one time, doing without some of that protection—it might make you think a lot more about it next time, that is, if there *was* a next time!"

"Huh? But we ain't at war with nobody!"

"The hell we ain't! I keep trying to tell you, boy, it's the same thing. When Bax sets his mind to do a thing, it's a sure enough war between him and anybody that gets in his way."

Rawley's men turned the wait into a fiesta, alternating between gluttonous feasting and sleeping when they were not on guard duty. Pilón uncovered a talent for cooking, once they had halted long enough to heat more than water for coffee. He put a kettle of pinto beans on the fire, adding a few strips of jerky, finely shredded, and rustled up some wild, onionlike plants which gave a different tang to the mixture. He found a handful of dried chile peppers upon rummaging through the dead Mando's pack and he added those to the pot.

Rawley had them moving early on the morning of the day they were to complete their task. He led them out and only Paco remained, guarding the remuda. They took three hours to make the drive to the ridge Tom had suggested. Once there, Rawley personally checked each wagon to make sure that it contained one hundred rifles and five thousand rounds of ammunition.

"Four hundred and ninety-two Spencers exactly," he said after making his count. "And maybe a thousand rounds left over. This will do very nicely. Biscuit, I want you to drive each wagon down in turn—you'll be able to see if they alter their arrangements during the exchange. If you see anything suspicious, anything at all, turn around and get out as fast as you can, understood?"

"I won't wait around," Biscuit promised.

"Riders over yonder!" Tom called out from the ridge. "Looks like he brought everybody in sight!"

Fergie, who had left his wagon to stand just below the crest of the ridge, moved up and looked over. Straining his eyes toward the point Tom indicated, he saw a flicker of movement and a little dust.

"Use my telescope," Rawley said, handing the instrument to Tom. "Watch me carefully, and when I wave my hat to you send one wagon out. They know the order in which to proceed; Biscuit will be driving each of them. If I start shooting do whatever you think best. And watch out for Corto—if he fires his wood, pull out to a more defensible position."

Rawley rode out alone to meet Don Eduardo and his men. Fergie watched and saw them meet about a half mile in front of the ridge where he stood.

"I propose that we complete the exchange one wagon at a time," Rawley said. "I have one hundred rifles per wagon, with ammunition. When you show me five thousand dollars I will signal for the wagon to move out. When you are satisfied with the merchandise you will hand over the money to me and we will proceed to the next wagon. Is that satisfactory?"

"Very satisfactory," Don Eduardo agreed. "Manuel, the treasure chest!"

A vaquero brought forward a burro and dismounted to unload a small dark wooden chest heavily reinforced with thick, wrought-iron straps. He heaved the box off the animal, grunting heavily, and dropped it to the ground. The box gave off a solid, reassuring chink when it hit the ground. The vaquero opened the chest and passed up a leather bag to Don Eduardo, who handed it on to Rawley.

"Five thousand American dollars," he said.

Rawley judiciously hefted the bag and then waved his left arm. He began counting the money and the first wagon came into view. By the time Biscuit had driven up to the waiting men and had unloaded the boxes, Rawley had assured himself that the bag contained exactly five thousand dollars. Don Eduardo motioned to one of his men, who stepped forward with a machete and began prying open the boxes. Don Eduardo himself lifted out each rifle, worked the action and replaced it in its nesting place. When he had tested each rifle and had dumped out the big sack of cartridges onto a stout woolen blanket, he nodded his approval. Rawley tossed the bag containing the money into Biscuit's wagon as he drove away.

They completed the transaction in that manner. Don Eduardo's men loaded the boxes of rifles onto a string of waiting burros, one box to each animal, and started them on their way as soon as each phase of the exchange had been completed. Rawley advised him that the last wagon contained only ninety-two rifles, due to the necessity of arming some of their own men; Don Eduardo removed twenty double eagles from the last sack before passing it over. They shook hands upon completing the transaction and rode away, each going in an opposite direction.

"Now to Parral!" Rawley shouted when he had rejoined his men and transferred all the money to a strongbox in one of the wagons.

CHAPTER SEVENTEEN

According to Rawley's estimate, they were some fifty miles south of Parral when they turned the rifles over to Don Eduardo. They took two days to cover that distance. Toward the end of the second day they saw evidence of that old mining town; a dirty gray cloud of smoke welled up from between two peaks and they aimed for it. Rawley located a wagon yard and led them to it. There he sold all the spare horses and mules, as well as the wagons, and also paid off his men. He handed Tom four hundred and fifty dollars and added a fifty-dollar bonus, explaining that this was their part of the sum he would have paid the hands who did not survive the long trip.

"It's down to us now," he said as Tom dropped the coins into his buckskin money bag and cinched it tight. I hope you'll see your way to going on with us."

"I sort of doubt it," Tom said. "I'd like to talk to some people first and see what kind of choices we've got. But we'll be around for a few days, so we'll be seeing you."

He and Fergie made an arrangement with the manager of the wagon yard, who agreed to stable their horses and hold their gear in a corner of his barn. They then set off for the business district, where they bought new clothing to replace worn-out garments, visited a bathhouse and barbershop and emerged looking considerably more respectable.

"Looks like you've growed a mite," Tom said as they tucked their dirty clothes, wrapped in a piece of newspaper, under an arm and walked away from the barbershop. "Ain't that the shirt you bought in San Antonio?"

"Yep, same one," Fergie agreed. "It *does* feel a little tight around the shoulders, I reckon. All that jerky and pinole must have agreed with me."

"It never hurt nobody. But it sure gets tiresome day after day."

"How about let's us finding an eating place? I'd sure love to be looking at a big plate of enchiladas and rice and beans!"

Parral had been built on a crossing of a small stream winding down out of the foothills of the Sierra Madres. The streets, like the stream, wound around the hills on either side of the watercourse and had more traffic than Fergie had ever seen in a Mexican town. Teamsters reined four- and six-horse wagons loaded with ore or mining supplies through the streets; smaller loads, carried on burros, bobbed up and down among the big wagons. Miners stood on every corner and cantinas emitted loud bursts of laughter and music. They saw quite as many Indians as Mexicans, as well as a sprinkling of men who were neither. They heard Spanish being spoken, the harsher guttural sounds of Indian dialects and even bits of languages which they took to be some European tongue.

"She's bubbling right along," Tom said as they stood for a moment in front of the restaurant where they had eaten. "Looks like everybody's really going great guns."

A whistle let out an ear-shattering blast and Fergie jumped nervously. The sound came from a complex of sheet-iron buildings high on a hill to the north of them. Looking up in that direction, Fergie saw a huge tower rising above the sheds.

"That'd be the tipple, or whatever they call it down here," Tom said. "See that big wheel up there in the top? They got a steam engine running that; it brings up the ore and lets the miners down. They might be digging away right now, a thousand or two thousand feet down from right where we're standing."

"Brrr! I can't feature doing that for a living! I'd be scared to death, being way down in the ground like that."

"Miners don't seem to mind it much. I knowed a feller in prison camp, he dug coal for a living back in Tennessee, I think it was. A lot of them fellers, they'd a lot rather go down in a mine and work ten or twelve hours than to try getting up on some of them wild ponies cowboys has to ride. I reckon it's all in what you been used to before."

"Well, I sure would hate to have to get used to that. Say, Uncle Tom, what are we going to do here? I mean, you said something about wanting to talk to some people; what about?"

"Well, if we're aiming to head up toward Chihuahua and El Paso, then we ought to know something about what's up that way. Indians? *Bandidos?* Dry stretches? Stuff like that. You ought not never to go charging into a place you don't know nothing about; there sure ain't nothing no more foolish."

"How about trying a blacksmith shop? A feller like that, he'd be likely to hear people talk about such things. Why, he might even know of some people fresh in town from up that way."

"Boy, you sure do come up with some good ideas sometimes," Tom drawled, looking at his nephew in surprise. "I was thinking about maybe finding a teamster but, damn my soul, I think you might have a better idea!"

They found a blacksmith's shop without difficulty. The owner painted them a very depressing picture, complete with oaths and flamboyant gestures, of the situation to the north. A band of Apaches had been terrorizing the area north of Chihuahua, he said, and the military detachment in the capital city had been fighting and chasing them for several weeks. Bandits capitalized upon the soldiers' difficulty and were having themselves a field day south of Chihuahua, where they could ride and plunder without fear of reprisal. The result of all this was that there was very little traffic between Parral and Chihuahua. A few wagon trains had gotten through, he said, but only those with heavily armed escorts.

"You reckon he was right about it being so bad up north of here?" Fergie asked after they had left the blacksmith.

"I know how we can find out: we can just keep on asking people. If they all say the same thing then we ought to believe it."

They spent the rest of the day wandering through Parral

and talking to everyone who looked as though he might be a teamster or have some knowledge of the freight business. They found a general agreement with the blacksmith's story: there was almost no traffic to or from the north. Most of the people accepted the situation, apparently, and were willing to wait until the bandits chose to move elsewhere or until the governor's troops were free to clear them out of the area.

CHAPTER EIGHTEEN

Tom and Fergie soon found that Rawley's plans were not at all affected by the troubles to the north of them. After deciding that Parral's two hotels did not look promising enough to warrant investing in a room, they went back to the wagon yard where they had left their horses and gear. The owner readily agreed to let them sleep in one of the wagons for fifty centavos. They were completing their bargain when Biscuit walked into the stone-walled enclosure.

"Thought I might find you here," he grunted.

"See anything out of Buffalo?" Tom asked.

"Sure enough. He come in with some wagons a couple or three days ago. Said he was right lucky to get here, too. Sounds like it just ain't nothing but meanness and mischief up north of here."

"So we've heard," Tom agreed, pulling a sour face.

"Look, why don't you fellers come on and eat supper with us tonight? Bax, he's got us holed up in a hotel where the fleas is pretty well trained—they check to see if you're asleep before they start biting. We'll have us a hell of a talking, all of us together."

Tom hesitated for only a moment before agreeing. They accompanied Biscuit up the street and followed him into an open gateway fronting a busy restaurant. Rawley and Frenchy beckoned them over to a big table under a vine-covered corner of the patio; Fergie saw two unfamiliar faces with them.

Buffalo Coleman looked to be about thirty, perhaps a little older. Of medium height and wiry in build, he was burned a deep shade of mahogany. His jet-black hair clung tightly to his skull in a mass of tight curls. A heavy Colt hung on his right hip and a big sheath knife balanced it on the left.

"This here's Red Shirt," he said, pointing to a very short, thick-chested Indian at his side.

"How do," Red Shirt grunted, gripping their hands tightly and giving each of them a ceremonial handshake.

"I hear nothing but bad news about conditions to the north of us," Rawley said as soon as they were all seated around the big table.

"The only good thing I heard was that there was still a north," Tom said. "Other than that I'd have to go along with you. What'd it look like to you, Buff?"

"It's a bear on both sides of Chihuahua," Coleman said; his voice was very deep and resonant. "We didn't have no trouble south of there but that's because we had us a little army. Coming down from El Paso, it was a little rougher. We had us a little set-to about two days north of there and lost a couple of men."

"Damn!" Tom snapped.

"Buffalo has been telling us more about our project," Rawley said. "From where we sit, Tom, that silver is only four days away!"

Tom said nothing. Fergie could see that he was irritated, but also more interested in their plans to go after the silver. Rawley changed the subject, however, and began questioning Coleman about New Mexico. Fergie found the talk boring after a time and turned his attention to Red Shirt.

He could not have guessed the man's age, though he clearly had many years on everyone else at the table. A lacework of wrinkles framed his black, glittering eyes; two deep furrows ran down beside his nostrils strongly outlined his cheekbones. His hair was still as black as a crow's back, though, and his appetite seemed good enough for a man far younger. Red Shirt ignored the talk and ate steadily, jaws working at the same steady pace.

Tom lapsed into a dark, sullen mood during the meal. Finally he stood up and pushed his chair back from the table. Fergie joined him and they walked back to the wagon yard.

"By damn, I got half a mind to throw in with them," he announced as they unrolled their blankets in one of the big wagons. "Here we went and busted a gut, almost, getting here and now we can't leave. I don't much think I'd like to sit around this place very long, either. What do you think?"

"You know, if we got us a piece of that silver it'd sure be nice," Fergie said. "I bet we could take it up into New Mexico or somewhere and get us a real pretty little place. You know, start all over again? I'm about to think I done me enough traveling for one lifetime."

"It's just like it was back there in San Antonio!" Tom grated, his voice shaking with fury. "We want to go off somewhere and mind our own damned business and what happens? Some damned reason or other pops up and we can't. Honest to God, boy, I'm starting to get mighty tired of us being pushed around!"

"Aw, maybe it wouldn't be so bad. If it started looking woolly we could always back out."

"Damn it, I reckon I'd just like to go with them boys! Hell, I figure it's a thousand to one we ain't going to find no silver, but I can't see no real good reason for missing the chance, even at them odds. And it's like you said: we could sure use that money, if there is any."

"Why don't we go, then? We ain't heard nobody say nothing about Indians up that way," Fergie urged. "Well, except for them Tarahumara, I mean, and they don't sound like they'd bother us. We sure won't be doing no good just sitting around here. And maybe by the time we get back they'll have all them *bandidos* run off. Either that or maybe somebody'll be putting a wagon train together."

"All right, we'll do it," Tom finally agreed. "I don't see how it could go wrong, I got to say that. We'll let them boys know about it tomorrow."

His decision did not bring him peace, Fergie noticed; he tossed restlessly in his blankets for hours. The next morning he awoke with a grim, haggard look but kept to his promise of the night before. Fergie could not understand his attitude, but he felt it would be wiser not to intrude on him. They dressed and rolled their blankets in silence, then went out in search of breakfast. After downing a few cups of coffee and putting away a plate of tortillas and warmed-over beans, they walked back out on the street and at once saw Frenchy.

"We might as well tell him we're going," Tom said. "I still don't like the idea much, but what the hell, maybe it'll beat laying around town."

"By damn, I knowed you wouldn't pass up a chance like this!" Frenchy crowed when Tom told him of their decision. "It's going to be just like the old days!"

"See? That's the thing about Frenchy," Tom said when the little man had scurried off to find Rawley. "He thinks them was good times. Biscuit, now, he knows a little better, but as long as Bax is around he'll foller him right up to the end."

"You really think they're all coming to a bad end, don't you?"

"Boy, it's just the plainest thing I ever seen. If ever there was a man made to be strung up by the neck, or maybe shot down like a dog, it's old Bax. What I'm afraid of is, we might be along when it comes his time. And things like that, they can sure be catching!"

"Well, it don't seem like much can go wrong on this trip. I mean, the Apaches don't fool around there much anymore, them other Indians don't bother you; maybe it'll come out all right."

"I hope so, I surely do."

They went back to the wagon yard and began inspecting their gear. Fergie decided that he needed a new cinch for his saddle and went off to buy one. When he got back his uncle was huddled with Rawley beside the wagon they had used for a bed the night before.

"Will you be ready to ride out of here tomorrow morning?" Rawley asked him when he squatted beside them.

"I'll be ready right now, just as soon as I get this cinch fastened on!"

"Hold on, there's no need for that big a hurry," Rawley said, smiling in his humorless way at the boy's enthusiasm. "That silver has been waiting there for twenty years and more; I suppose it can wait another day or two."

They agreed to meet at the same restaurant for dinner that

night, where they would make their final plans. Tom and Fergie spent a few more hours in checking their gear and horses and in laying in a store of supplies for the trek into the mountains. Two horses needed shoeing; they took them to a blacksmith shop next to the wagon yard and talked the farrier into doing the work that afternoon.

They rode west out of Parral an hour after sunrise the next morning. Fergie and Tom had thrown packs on two of their horses; Rawley and his men had three packhorses. Fergie herded the extra mounts, following the others.

By the end of the first day they were heading downhill. Fergie saw a vast, broad plain opening out before them, but on its far side, some fifteen miles away, he saw another and even more imposing line of mountains that promised to dwarf the range they had just passed.

"That first batch of hills, they was just to get you warmed up good for the second line," Biscuit said when he rode back to help gather the horses for the night. "I can't make out if that Indian intends to get up into the middle of them or not."

"He don't seem like he wants to talk anybody's ear off," Fergie noted.

"Old Buffalo, he can get a few words out of him, but I ain't seen nobody else that can get him going."

"Did you ever make out just why it is he's so willing to come down here with us and show us where that silver is? What's he up to, anyhow?"

"Buff says he thinks the old codger wants to come down here to die. Yep, I know it's a harebrained idea, but Buff claims the old man was born up in them mountains somewhere. He reckons the old feller has it in his mind to leave this old world at the same place where he come into it. It sounds plumb crazy to me, but Buff, he says it sounds pretty Indian to him."

"It might be," Fergie admitted. "I always heard that Indians was apt to do things like that. But I never had nothing to do with them, so I can't say for sure about it."

They continued across the valley the next day and brought up against the higher range of mountains. Red Shirt turned his pony north and led them along the side of the valley. He seemed to be searching for a particular trail, passing by three trails that led up into the peaks at his left. They rode up onto a low ridge that gave them an excellent view of the valley and camped for the night. Looking off to the north, Fergie caught a glimpse of a glittering white pile of masonry.

"Nonoanave," Red Shirt grunted when it was pointed out to him.

"What was that?" Rawley asked, overhearing the word.

"Nonoanave," the Indian repeated. "Tarahumara."

Rawley still could not understand the cryptic remark and asked Buffalo for a fuller statement. Coleman spoke to the old man in Apache, mixing in a few Spanish words, and said they were looking at a Tarahumara Indian town called Nono-anave. The white structure they saw was a Jesuit mission church.

"Tarahumara," Fergie said. "Somebody in Parral mentioned them. They're the ones who can run all day, that feller claimed."

"But they ain't like the Apaches," Tom added, for Rawley's benefit. "It's mostly live and let live with them."

"How much farther north do we have to go?" Rawley demanded.

"One day, maybe," Coleman reported after another consultation with Red Shirt. "And then one or two days into the mountains. He says they used to have a lot of fun shooting up the Tarahumara in the old days. They was cowards, couldn't fight, he claims."

"If they was such all-fired cowards," Tom grumbled, "how come they're still here and it's the Apaches who moved up north? That don't sound quite right to me!"

"Perhaps our friend's opinion has an element of wishful thinking in it," Rawley suggested. "Or it might be that he sees it in the same light as a colonel from Louisiana I once knew. According to him his regiment never lost a battle. There were a few times, however, when the battle ended before he had won it!"

Red Shirt paid no attention to their criticisms of his view;

indeed, no one was certain that he even understood what they were saying. Coleman claimed that the old man knew a little English and somewhat more Spanish, though he said nothing in either language to any of them. Fergie tried a few observations in Spanish from time to time, but mostly the Indian ignored him completely.

The country through which they passed was inhabited, though they saw few people. Fergie came upon an occasional building as he trailed after the remuda, which ranged well off the trail used by the others. The buildings looked more like granaries than dwellings, and some had small piles of knobby, flinty ears of corn. Built of flat, unmortared stones and roughly shaped branches stacked to form a kind of lattice-work wall, the little huts—most were no more than six or eight feet square—had no doors or windows.

Corn grew in small patches hacked into the valley floor. The stalks looked runty and starved, even to an unskilled eye like Fergie's; they reared up in a shabby disarray that made little attempt at looking like rows. Fergie saw one man during their trek up the valley. The man wore a loose, shirtlike garment which appeared to be folded between his legs, like a diaper, and nothing else except a headband; he stood beside a thick patch of junipers three hundred yards off and watched as Fergie spurred toward the horses to keep them out of another small patch of corn.

They awoke the next morning to find themselves in a thick fog which restricted their visibility to a maximum of forty yards. Red Shirt paid no attention to the fog. He led them out at a walk and followed the same winding trail they had been on the day before. They proceeded for about four hours, making slow time, and stopped when the trail branched. One segment bent slightly to the right, or toward the east; the other turned left at a sharp angle. Red Shirt slid off his horse and looked at the trails, then off into the fog. Coleman stepped down from his horse and went over to the old man.

"He thinks this is the place but he ain't sure," Coleman reported after exchanging a few words with the Indian. "He wants to wait till it clears up enough for him to get a look around us."

"He knows where he's going," Rawley said. "We seem to have no choice in the matter."

They pulled off the trail and dismounted, all except for Biscuit; he went back to look for Fergie. He had kept the horses close to the trail, since the fog would have made it easy to get lost, and was not far behind. They set up a temporary camp under a grove of oak trees and waited. After a couple more hours the fog lifted, or rather, it was more nearly dissolved by a heavy mist. A damp chill began settling into all of them.

The mist continued and occasionally thickened into a genuine rain. The only satisfying moment of their halt came when Red Shirt took advantage of a momentary lull in the drizzle to survey their surroundings. He saw enough to decide they had come to the right place; the trail leading up into the mountains was the one they sought, he told Coleman.

"Near as I can make out you go up that left-hand fork there," Coleman reported after his conference with the old Apache, "and go up that little canyon there till you get onto a kind of saddle between two peaks. There's a big canyon on the other side of that saddle—he says it's a whopper. We got to go down in it to get to where they dumped the silver. He reckons it's about a day and a half or two days from here, what with us hauling them packhorses and all."

"A canyon in there?" Rawley asked, looking up at the peaks towering over them. "It doesn't seem very likely, does it? We'll have to see if perhaps something didn't get lost in the translation!"

They stayed in their makeshift camp until midafternoon. The mist showed no sign of abating; rather, it became heavier. Rawley eyed the thickening clouds with disgust.

"Let's ride into that village and test the Jesuits' hospitality," he said.

They set off and rode into Nonoanave a short time later. Rawley led them up to the church, which looked even more imposing when viewed at close range. A tall, black-robed man emerged from one of the smaller rock buildings beside it.

"Welcome to Nonoanave Mission," he said in Spanish when they had ridden up in front of him. "I am Father Ciro."

"We were wondering if there were someplace in town where we could sleep tonight," Tom said after Rawley had tried English and drew an apologetic smile and a shrug from the priest. "Someplace that's dry."

"We have no guest quarters as such," the priest replied, frowning as he concentrated. "There are almost no travelers through this region, you know. I suppose the driest place would be our stables; they are empty since we have given up keeping horses. Come, I will show you."

He led them to another cluster of buildings at the back of the church. A line of stables, made of neatly mortared stone and covered with stout shingles, made another wing to the complex of buildings. There was even a stone-walled corral.

"It is a poor accommodation," Father Ciro said as he showed them the stalls, all neatly swept out. "But they are as dry as any place in the village. And remember, such a place served as the birthplace for our blessed Savior!"

He left after requesting them to avoid all contact with the Indians and showing them a stack of dry wood in one stall. The men quickly unsaddled and threw off the packs, then turned the horses into the corral. Frenchy soon had a fire going and they began brewing a pot of coffee.

They caught an occasional glimpse of an Indian moving around the church but none ventured very near the stables. Fergie went out to check the horses once more as darkness spread through the valley; he stuffed his pistol into the front of his trousers before leaving the stalls. As he stood beside the gate—actually it was a series of limbs jammed into notches and slots in the mortared gateposts—he heard a noise to his right, at the very end of the stables. Looking that way, he caught a glimpse of a form ducking around the corner.

He could not identify the man but he had a definite impression that he was wearing a broad-brimmed hat, an item of clothing he had seen on no one except his own party. His

curiosity fully aroused, he decided to investigate. He advanced
to the corner of the stables and peered around them. A ragged
cluster of huts lay a few yards away; there were no other buildings nearby and he saw no trace of the man. After standing
there for a moment and wondering what to do he decided to
investigate further.

He cautiously advanced upon the huts, all of which were of
the stone and log construction he had seen earlier on the
primitive corncribs. They had a rundown look and seemed to
be vacant. He moved alongside them, stepping carefully and
making as little noise as possible. As he neared the end of
the cluster he heard a muffled cry, short and high-pitched; it
sounded as though it came from one of them. He moved
closer to the hut from which he thought the sound had come
and paused beside it.

At first he could hear nothing. Then his ears caught the
rasp of labored breathing and a few gasps. Edging toward the
narrow, open doorway, he hesitated a moment and drew his
pistol before looking inside. For a moment he could see nothing, owing to the darkness, but then he made out two forms.

One, definitely Indian, lay on the dirt floor of the hut. He
saw a flash of steel against the Indian's throat and recognized
it as a knife. Then he saw that the form was that of a girl; she
wore the gaudy calico blouse and the voluminously pleated
skirt he had seen on the women of the village.

"Just you get them legs spread out there, honey, and give us
a ride," he heard, at once recognizing Coleman's exception-
ally deep voice. "You'll go crazy about it before you even know
what's happening!"

Fergie stiffened with surprise. He saw Coleman flip up the
girl's skirts, caught a glimpse of coppery thighs gleaming in
the half-light. Coleman kneed her thighs apart, fumbling at
the front of his trousers as he did so, and then leaned over her.
Her cry, sharp but low and quavering with fear, jarred Fergie
out of his surprised immobility.

"Get off that girl!" he snarled, stepping into the room and
cocking his pistol.

The click-clack of the Colt's hammer being thumbed back echoed around the walls like thunder, or so it seemed to him

"What the . . . !" Coleman grunted, rearing up. "Why, you little whelp, get on back to your damned horses!"

"Like hell I will," Fergie said. He moved out of the doorway and dropped to one knee, aiming the pistol carefully. "Get the hell off'n her or I'll blow your head off!"

Coleman hesitated only a moment before lurching up from the girl. He hefted the knife, obviously wanting to drive it deep into Fergie's stomach, but the muzzle of the youth's pistol followed his every move.

"Drop that knife right now," Fergie warned. "You even look like you want to throw it and I'll blast you!"

Coleman shrugged and tossed the knife aside. The girl pulled her skirts down and retreated into a corner, whimpering and snuffling. Fergie moved aside and motioned for Coleman to go through the doorway. Just then they heard the thump of running, booted feet outside. Fergie edged back against the wall but continued to watch Coleman carefully.

"What's going on in here?" Rawley asked, peering inside and spotting them.

"I seen somebody sneaking around the stables and when I got out here I found him and this girl," Fergie said. "He had a knife at her throat and he was about to . . . well, you know."

"I thought as much," Rawley snapped. "Buffalo, you utter, absolute fool! Button up your trousers; you look like the village idiot with that thing hanging out! By God, I ought to geld you myself!"

"Hell, she's just an Indian," Coleman protested, though Fergie noted that he was quick to rearrange his clothing. "Bax, it won't do no—"

"Shut up! Of all the people in the world, why should I take *your* advice? Get on back with the others before I change my mind and kill you here and now!"

Coleman scooped up his knife and hurried through the doorway. Rawley stepped out of the hut and watched him leave. At that moment a group of Indian men, six or seven in all, came around one of the huts. Rawley motioned to Fergie and they left.

"Don't hurry and don't dawdle," Rawley told him. "I'm not sure what kind of trouble that fool has gotten us into but it won't do to let them see that we're worried."

"I didn't know what to do," Fergie muttered. "But damn it, it didn't seem right just to stand there and let him . . . well, do it."

"You did exactly right. I would not have blamed you if you had shot him. That sort of thing could endanger the entire purpose of our trip. I warn you, though, you'd best watch yourself from now on—Coleman is mean and he will not take this lightly."

"I'll watch it," Fergie promised.

Tom pulled him to one side when they returned and demanded the full story. Fergie gave it to him as best he could. Tom grunted from time to time, looking more and more incredulous; he pushed his hat back and shook his head slowly when Fergie had finished his tale.

"Lord, Lord, my own nephew!" he murmured wonderingly. "Boy, don't you know that old Buff has killed men for a lot less than that?"

"Well, it just seemed like the right thing to do," Fergie said, gulping nervously. "I reckon I didn't think much about it at the time, or maybe I'd have backed off and let him go on with it."

"Oh, it was probably the right thing," Tom acknowledged, "but I ain't so sure it was the *best* thing. We're going to have to watch out for you. That Buff, he holds a grudge pretty good."

Tom motioned for Fergie to stay where he was and walked over to the others. He squatted down beside the fire, directly across from Coleman.

"Well, Buff, it looks like you ran into a wildcat here," Tom said, breaking the heavy silence. When Coleman ignored him, except for directing a surly look his way, he went on. "I reckon you'll be feeling a mite angry toward Fergie. Well, I'm telling you here and now, don't let it go no further than feeling. Anything happens to that boy, I'll nail you up myself."

"Go to hell!" Coleman growled. "Damfool kid that can't mind his own business, he needs to be learnt some manners."

"That might be, but don't think that anybody's appointing you to do the learning!"

"That's enough of that kind of talk," Rawley snapped. "We don't have enough men to lose any because of quarreling. And now . . . who knows what might happen?"

CHAPTER NINETEEN

Rawley and his men did little sleeping that night. The village's inhabitants had gathered near the building from which Father Ciro emerged to greet the visitors. Occasional shouts broke the night's stillness, leaving little doubt that the Indians were strongly aroused. Rawley had his men bring the horses from the corral and put them in the stalls; they could watch the gate from their shelter, but the stone walls of the corral, only five feet high, offered no real protection from a village of aroused Indians.

"Hell, I ain't standing no guard without no gun or knife!" Coleman protested when Rawley told him to take up an exposed position at the end of the stables nearest the church, and to do so unarmed. "Why, it's *me* they want!"

"Exactly, and don't think I'm not considering letting them have you!" Rawley purred. "At the moment, though, I think your worth to us justifies some effort. That could change, however. And if you're unarmed, well, that might keep you more alert. I certainly will not trust you with weapons, so get out there and be quick about it!"

They kept an uneasy watch until sunrise. The day dawned clear and chilly with no trace of the clouds and rain which had plagued them the day before. Rawley had them begin saddling their horses and throwing the packs onto the packhorses as soon as there was enough light to see; they stripped the nonessentials out of their packs and tied the hitches down extra firmly. He whistled in the guards, but before they could get moving Father Ciro and another black-robed priest led a horde of Indians around the corner of the church. Some of the Indians carried sticks, but as he looked them over

Fergie could see no rifles or pistols. He breathed considerably easier at that.

"Keep your distance!" Rawley called out when the group had advanced to a point some forty yards away from the stables.

Tom repeated the command in Spanish, suspecting that no one in the crowd understood so much as a word of English.

"One of your men has committed a grave and despicable crime against our people!" Father Ciro called out.

"That may be, but I cannot afford to give him up to you," Rawley said when Tom had translated for him. "I need him for our trip into the mountains."

"He committed the crime here and he must stand trial here," Father Ciro stubbornly insisted.

"Padre, we're riding out of here," Rawley said. "I'm sorry for what happened but I'll not give up one of my men. If you try to stop us we'll ride right over you!"

He motioned for Biscuit and Frenchy to take up positions at one flank, so they could guard their rear as they rode out past the huts where Fergie had surprised Coleman with the girl.

"Get the horses out!" he shouted to Fergie. "Drive them west; we'll catch up with you!"

Fergie yelled at the animals, which had been gathered into two of the end stalls, and herded them away from the church. Already nervous and edgy, they galloped away quickly and stayed in a compact bunch. Fergie held his breath as they sped away; he knew that they had tied the packs down extra firmly but he also knew that no diamond hitch ever thrown by man would stand up to the stresses of a running horse for very long.

When Father Ciro stepped forward again, moving as if to cut off the escape route of those remaining, Rawley drew one of his pistols. The priest continued his march forward and Rawley fired, planting a bullet squarely between his sandaled feet and kicking up the hem of his robe. Father Ciro hesitated a moment, and his face, dark with stubble and drawn with tension, went pale. After a moment he resumed his march forward.

Rawley thumbed back the hammer of his pistol and fired again. This time he sent a ball into the man's right shoulder. He deliberately aimed high and far enough to the side to miss any vital organs. The bullet knocked the priest sprawling. A dead silence fell over the throng as the second priest bent over Father Ciro and began pulling his robe aside to examine the wound.

"We mean to leave here and we'll kill anyone who tries to stop us," Rawley shouted. "Coleman, Tom, move out! Take the Apache with you. Frenchy, you and Biscuit guard our rear; I'll help you. Move!"

The villagers' indecision gave Rawley and his men just the opening they needed. Some of the Indians plainly wanted to rush them but most knelt around the fallen priest. Tom led the way, riding out at a gallop, and the others followed closely.

Fergie had begun trying to bring the remuda and pack-horses to a slower pace as soon as they had cleared the village and he saw that there was no pursuit. As nearly as he could tell none of the packs had come loose. He felt very exposed and alone; the sight of his uncle and the others galloping out of the village, perhaps a half mile away, caused him to heave a great sigh of relief.

"Tell him to find that trail up into those mountains," Rawley shouted to Coleman, riding beside Red Shirt.

"Look!" Tom called out, pointing behind and to their left.

They saw six Indians, almost antlike at that distance, moving out of the village at a long, graceful pace that was probably as fast as a horse's trot. Red Shirt watched them for a moment before shaking his shaggy head and grunting something to Coleman.

"He says we're in for it now!" Coleman called out, his tone incredulous. "And he really means it, too!"

"What can they do?" Rawley demanded, his voice sharp and skeptical. "I didn't see so much as a single gun in the entire village. I don't believe they even have bows and arrows!"

They continued toward the junction of the trails which Red
Shirt had marked the day before. As he herded the remuda
up the branch leading into the mountains, Fergie saw the
grove under which they had temporarily camped the day before. He could not help wishing they had stayed there; he
would gladly have endured the cold and dampness if they
could have avoided the trouble at the village.

Red Shirt led them along the other branch of the trail and
up a canyon cutting directly into the big range of mountains.
The canyon's floor rose steeply. Wagon-sized boulders and
dead trees, thrown into a rat's nest by flooding waters, littered
the way; there was a very narrow trail winding among the
debris, but they spent almost as much time in riding from side
to side as they did in moving forward.

All of them spotted Indians from time to time as they advanced. The Tarahumara evidently had a series of foot trails
leading up either side of the canyon and did not have to rely
on the trail Rawley and his group had to take. They made
little effort to hide themselves and came no closer than about
one hundred yards.

"Hell, there's dozens of them!" Biscuit exclaimed.

"Now, I bet there's another village up ahead," Frenchy
objected. "Probably they're both on the warpath now."

Fergie knew better. The first Indian he had been able to
see clearly carried a blanket slung over one shoulder and
cinched around his waist. The blanket was of a rich, chocolate
hue and had a creamy stripe running along its length. No
other Indian that he had seen carried a blanket of any sort.
Several times that day Fergie looked up and saw that same
blanket, always a little ahead of him and to the right.

"Looks like that feller in Parral might have been right,"
Tom said when Fergie told him that night of seeing the same
man throughout the day. "I reckon them Indians *can* run all
day!"

"What's this?" Rawley asked, overhearing their exchange.

He cocked a coldly skeptical eye at Fergie as he repeated
his words. Tom reinforced the report by telling him what they
had heard in Parral.

"It doesn't seem possible that people could perform such feats," Rawley muttered. "But I must admit that I saw no Indians with blankets, either. Here, I'll see what our Apache friend has to say."

Rawley questioned Red Shirt through Coleman; the Indian told them that almost any Tarahumara male could maintain that peculiar, loping pace all day, even adding in a few brief spurts of faster running if it were needed. They could be outrun on fairly level ground, he said, but you would probably kill most of your horses in doing so; in rough country they could not be left behind. Their strategy was a simple one: they pursued until the enemy dropped from exhaustion, then closed in to administer the final blows with clubs, rocks and knives. They also used slings with considerable effect, being fairly accurate up to thirty or forty yards.

"It doesn't sound like such a poor strategy when you think about it," Rawley mused. "They seem to be making good use of what advantages they have. Ask him why he has such a low opinion of them."

"He says they're all women," Coleman reported after conferring again with the Apache. "They go in for farming, they let priests tell them what to do, they don't even go after the Mexicans."

"It would appear that our guide's standards are not our own," Rawley said. "We are into it now, it seems; now we must see what we can make of it all."

"You aiming to keep going on up into them mountains?" Tom asked.

"We are much too close to that silver to back out now," Rawley replied.

"According to that Apache, they're more likely to keep up with us if we stay in this rough country," Tom pointed out.

"Nevertheless, we'll go on," Rawley insisted.

Red Shirt broke his customary silence to speak. They were all startled; it was the first time since leaving Parral that he had volunteered so much as a word.

"He wants to know what's all the fuss about?" Coleman

said. "The way he sees it, we're all made to die and this is the best place in the world for it to happen."

"I reckon I got me a sight more living to do," Tom grunted. "Not that this ain't mighty pretty country, but I ain't figuring on staying here forever!"

They spent a very anxious night. Rawley kept four of them awake at all times; no one got to sleep more than about three hours. Red Shirt told them that the Tarahumara had no fear of fighting during darkness, in contrast to most Indians. The were no assaults during the night but an occasional stone came whistling into their midst. One thudded to earth near Fergie and rolled against his foot; he picked it up and found that it was easily as large as a hen's egg. He put in in his pocket and showed it to his uncle the next morning.

"I sure do hope old Red Shirt was wrong about them being able to hit anything with their slings," he said, producing the large, smoothly rounded stone. "You get one of these up against the side of your head and that might be the end of it right there!"

"By damn, I sure wish Bax had let them Indians have old Buff," Tom growled. "I don't mind telling you, boy, this looks to me like it's a sure enough tight spot. I'd be willing to turn around and head back, except we might be even worse off with just the two of us going."

The Indians became more aggressive during that morning as they sought to trap the men in the head of the canyon. The trail led up to a huge rock slide that blocked the way completely; they would have to follow a narrow ledge that zigzagged its way up the wall. The Tarahumara had concentrated most of their men there and loosed a perfect hail of stones as Frenchy, in the point, neared the slide. They quickly retreated out into the open part of the canyon, where they had somewhat more protection from the flying stones.

"You sure won't be able to ride up that trail," Frenchy reported. "Hell, we might even be lucky just to walk up it, the way they're flinging them rocks!"

"Tom, you and Biscuit take up a position over there and there," Rawley ordered, pointing out locations. "Use your rifles to protect Frenchy and me; we'll try the trail. If we can get on top we ought to be able to fire down on them and take the pressure off for the rest of you. Buff, you and the Indian go up next. Fergie, get the horses up after them. Good shooting!"

Coleman and Red Shirt drew their own rifles and levered off a few rounds as Frenchy and Rawley spurred up to the rock slide, dismounted and began working their way up the trail. They were only indifferent marksmen, though their bullets probably helped keep the Indians above from concentrating all their energy on the two climbing men. Tom and Biscuit scored a hit each, drawing fierce screams from their victims; after that the volume of stones decreased markedly.

Once Rawley and Frenchy reached the top of the canyon wall and got their rifles into action, they were able to drive the Indians to cover. Coleman and Red Shirt found it easy work indeed to work their way up the trail. Fergie had a difficult time getting the remuda started up the forbidding trail, but once the first couple of horses had proceeded partway the others proved to be much more amenable to his directions. Red Shirt gathered them into a compact bunch as they lumbered over the top of the canyon wall. Tom and Biscuit then ascended the trail, taking turns covering each other as they advanced.

They came out onto a broad, grassy mesa once they left the canyon's rim. The mesa stretched for at least a mile on both sides and to the front. To the left, or south, another steep slope led up the side of a rock-studded mountain; the northern edge of the mesa appeared to fall off into another series of jumbled canyons. Ahead, to the west, another line of mountains appeared far off, and Fergie supposed that the mesa dropped down slightly as it approached them.

Red Shirt led them due west across the mesa for a little more than half its breadth, then began angling off to the north. It soon became apparent to all of them that the Indians had not concentrated all their forces beside the canyon wall. To the north and south, along both sides of the mesa, they spotted small figures moving ahead with that all too familiar pace.

"By damn, they sure ain't much for wearing down!" Biscuit growled.

Gradually, as they edged closer to the western edge of the mesa, they could begin to see that it dropped off into a tremendous chasm. None of them had time to examine the abyss, naturally, but it gave every indication of dwarfing anything they had ever seen before. Fergie darted occasional glimpses into the vastness to his left as he clattered along behind the horses; he could see mountain peaks swimming in a sea of mist and occasional patches of blue-green vegetation far below.

"*Barranca del Cobre,*" Red Shirt grunted that evening when they made camp beside the chasm.

"Copper Canyon," Tom said for Rawley's benefit. "Well, I reckon she's a booger, sure enough!"

"It's incredible," Rawley murmured. "A pity we cannot take the time to admire it properly!"

"I seen a lot in my time," Biscuit said, gazing into the canyon as he ate pinole from his cupped palm, "but I sure never expected to see anything like that!"

Rawley pressed Red Shirt for another estimate about their nearness to the silver; he was told that they would come to a trail leading down into the canyon tomorrow and should be at the spot where the silver had been dumped by midafternoon. The Tarahumara were becoming more aggressive and had edged up fairly close to their camp as night fell upon them. An occasional stone, lobbed high, came tumbling down near them, and they all felt extremely nervous. Fergie was left to guard the packs with Red Shirt as soon as the darkness had enclosed them; Rawley led the others out on a patrol aimed at making the Indians pull back farther.

They wriggled out in darkness, each man armed with only a pistol and a knife. Fergie looked around nervously; a flicker of firelight far off in the distance to the east. Other winking lights appeared farther to the north.

"Tarahumara."

"Huh?" he grunted, startled nearly out of his wits by the word from Red Shirt.

"Tarahumara fires," the old Apache repeated. "Signal others. Soon many Tarahumara, all goddamn mad. Big goddamn fight."

Fergie said nothing for a moment. The old man had spoken in fairly good Spanish, throwing in English oaths; his wheezing, rasping voice made it difficult to understand all his words clearly.

"They'll kill us tomorrow?" he finally asked.

"Kill some. You stay?"

"Where could I go?"

"Trail to Casas Grandes, Janos that way," Red Shirt said, pointing to the northeast. "See peak like moon, keep there. Follow creek, easy. Tarahumara no follow."

"Why don't we all go that way, then?"

"Buffalo Man damned fool; Bullet Eyes greedy. All die soon."

Fergie thought that over carefully. "Buffalo Man" was Coleman, obviously, but "Bullet Eyes"? Then he thought of Rawley—the man's eyes did indeed have a bulletlike quality, somehow; he decided it was mostly a matter of their being so devoid of all expression.

"What about you?" he asked.

"I come here to die."

Fergie could think of nothing to say to that. The old man's voice had an air of finality about it, as though he had said the last word on the subject. The youth got to his feet and shuffled about for a moment. He looked around and noticed that the fires were burning only to the north and east; there was not a flicker of light to the south.

"Plenty Tarahumara there," Red Shirt said, noticing the youth's look. Then, turning and gesturing again to the north, he said, "Not so many there."

"It's a trick? They're trying to scare us into going south?"

Red Shirt nodded and fell back into his customary silence, refusing to say another word. A shot rang out a moment later, blending into a shrill cry of pain; then two more shots blasted the silence. Fergie's eye caught two of the muzzle blasts and he saw that they had not come from the same gun.

"Fergie?" he heard his uncle call a few moments later.

"Over here!" he replied.

The four men made their way back to the little cluster of horses and packs. They agreed that they had hit at least one Indian, perhaps two, and that their sally had caused the attackers to fall back.

"Hey, that's right!" Fergie exclaimed. "I ain't heard any rocks come in here in the last two or three minutes!"

"That will be enough to let them know that we are not to be trifled with," Rawley said. "Perhaps it will convince them to keep their distance."

Fergie found himself standing beside Biscuit just before dawn; they had moved around onto the far side of the remuda to guard against a sneak attack on the horses from that angle. A sickle-thin moon gave enough light for them to be able to watch for interlopers, who would have to cross at least fifty yards of short grass to get at the herd.

"You know, I'm starting to wonder if maybe old Bax ain't bit hisself off a real mouthful here," Biscuit observed. "Them Indians, they act like they mean business for certain."

"Maybe we'll be able to shake loose from them tomorrow, once we get started down into that canyon," Fergie suggested, speaking in a very low whisper.

"Hell, speak up there, boy—ain't no use in trying to fool them; they know where we're at," Biscuit said, chuckling wryly. "And here's one mother's son that ain't going down into no canyon, not with no pack of upset Indians behind him and yelping for blood at every step!"

"Why not? Lordy, from the looks of that hole, you could just about lose your own shadder down there!"

"You might could if you got to the bottom," Biscuit agreed. "But getting there, boy, that's the tough spot. All they got to do, don't you see, is to sit up there on that rim and start bouncing a few boulders and logs over the side, and then what happens to them that's on the trail down below? Huh?"

His remark brought Fergie up short, showing him a danger he had not appreciated before. He saw at once that the man was right. No doubt the trail leading down into the depths of the canyon was a narrow, winding one—probably it was very much like the one they had used to climb out of the canyon at the other side of the mesa—and they would have almost no space in which to maneuver around projectiles hurled from above. Even if they managed to dodge most of the boulders, surely some of them would start a rock slide and—he had no heart for thinking through the rest of it.

"You know, that canyon don't look so very good after all!" Fergie said, fighting to keep his voice under control.

"Nope, it sure don't, but that's where Bax is bound and determined for us to go. He's more set on getting at that silver than anything I ever seen."

"By damn, I think I'd be ready to sign over my part to them Indians right now if they'd just let us ride on out of here in one piece!"

"Yessiree, you and me both. But that ain't the way you play this game. Them Indians, they don't care squat about that silver; they just want Buff's hide. And Bax's too, I reckon, for shooting that padre down the way he did. Hell's afire, boy, they might want to get *all* of us, for that matter! I tell you what, Fergie, if one of them Indians gets me, you just glom onto them saddlebags of mine, hear? I got me my share out of what we made off'n them rifles; if they dent my old skull up with one of them rocks they're so damned good at flinging, she's all yours!"

"Aw, we'll probably get out some way or another."

Fergie wanted to tell Biscuit what Red Shirt had said about the trail leading off to the northeast, and the likelihood that it was only weakly guarded, but he did not. He feared that Biscuit would think that he was proposing for them to leave the others and try to save themselves; he was not about to be thought capable of suggesting so cowardly a deed. Instead he decided to wait until he could mention the matter to his uncle, who would not make such a mistake about him.

CHAPTER TWENTY

Fergie pulled his uncle aside the next morning as they saddled up and waited for enough light to ride. He told him of his conversation with Red Shirt and also about Biscuit's fears concerning the descent into the canyon.

"Biscuit's right about that," Tom said, narrowing his eyes thoughtfully. "They could start a hell of a ruckus from up on top and there wouldn't be a blessed thing we could do about it. Now, this old Indian just up and started talking out of the blue, did he?"

"Like to scared me to death," Fergie admitted. "I mighta missed some of what he was saying but I think I got just about all of it straight."

"It makes some sense, you know. They wouldn't be the first people to try scaring somebody into walking right into a trap. I wonder about that Apache, though—why would he start wanting to help us out all of a sudden? I just don't know about it. What do you think? You reckon it's time to pull out?"

"Damn, I don't know, Uncle Tom, I surely don't! If you think Biscuit was right about them having the top hand once we got started down into that canyon, then . . . well, I don't know either. It'd sure be bad, backing out on people after you've sided with them, but if all you was doing was giving them some company to die with, then what's the point?"

Tom did not say directly that they would try the trail but he looked around with a new confidence, as if the mere existence of an escape hatch, however dubious it might be, were enough to stiffen his resolve.

"Biscuit, you and the kid get the horses lined out along

the trail," Rawley ordered when there was enough light to move. "We'll cover your rear. The Indian says we have two or three more hours before we get to his trail down into the canyon, so don't go all out. Save something back."

Fergie and Biscuit got the spare mounts and packhorses under way. The hard pace of the last two days was already beginning to tell on the horses, despite their having changed mounts regularly during the day; they were a trifle sluggish and slow to obey.

Firing broke out as soon as they pulled up into their saddles. The Tarahumara mounted an assault when they saw the men preparing to mount. They dashed forward, running a few paces and then dropping to the grass for a moment; behind them a battery of braves loosed a rain of stones with their slings. There was still enough darkness to make aiming uncertain, but Rawley and Coleman each hit a brave. The assault quickly melted away but the stones continued to pelt down among them. Frenchy took an egg-sized stone on the point of his left shoulder; he bellowed with pain and staggered against his horse.

"By God, my arm's broke!" he moaned. "Ooohh, I can't even move it!"

"You'll live," Rawley said, going over and knotting the ends of the man's reins together. "And you can still shoot with your right hand, and you'd better be ready to do just that!"

They pulled up into their saddles and rode off, snapping off a few last shots at the howling Indians, and almost at that moment Fergie got a very personal taste of warfare. He and Biscuit had gotten the horses under way smoothly and had them moving off in a compact bunch. Fergie fell behind slightly as the firing continued; he looked back to see what was happening.

"They'll be all right," Biscuit yelled to him. "Stick with these horses!"

Fergie threw one last look at his uncle and the other men and then turned back to the remuda. As he was spurring up to resume his place beside the horses, he saw an Indian rise up from a little gully cutting across the mesa. The man rose to his feet and in the same smooth, graceful motion hurled a lance toward Biscuit, who was about thirty feet away.

"Look out!" he yelled.

Biscuit saw the man but could not move in time to dodge the short, flint-tipped lance. It struck him in the left side, entering just below the ribs, and angled up into his chest cavity. Fergie drew his pistol from its saddle holster, cocked it and swerved directly toward the Indian, who was drawing a knife from his belt. He waited until he was almost upon the man and fired from a distance of no more than fifteen feet. His bullet struck the Indian squarely in the chest and toppled him over backward. Fergie rode on toward Biscuit, who was drooping weakly over his saddlehorn. Fergie pulled up beside him just in time to catch him as he fell from the saddle. The lance had worked itself free and had fallen from his body, leaving a gaping wound. Biscuit's shirt and trousers were covered with blood and his face had turned a dead, sickly shade of gray.

"B-b-boy, I'm . . . sorry I got you into this," he muttered as Fergie eased him to the ground.

"It wasn't your fault," Fergie said, wondering what he should do next.

"No, it ain't that way. Th-th-that feller in San Antone—he ain't dead!"

"Huh?"

"Tom just knocked him out," Biscuit gasped weakly. "Me and Bax, we figured—*ugghh*—we figured you'd *have* to go along with us if . . . if we said he was a goner. I seen him on the streets the day before we left; he didn't have no more than a b-b-black eye!"

Fergie could not speak. Biscuit reached up, grasping at his wrist, and tried to say something else; the effort turned into a gasping wheeze and he fell backward. His eyes gazed sightlessly into the brightening sky.

"Fergie! Is he done for?" Tom yelled, riding up and skidding to a halt beside them. Getting no answer, he leaped down and felt of Biscuit's left wrist. "He's gone; come on, let's move it!"

"No, hang on a minute!" Fergie blurted out. "Wait, Uncle Tom, he told me something. You know that Phillips, back in San Antonio? Biscuit said he wasn't dead at all!"

"Huh? Wasn't dead?"

"No! Him and Rawley just made that up. Honest, that's what he said! He told me that they done it so's you and me'd be scared to go on by ourselves, so we'd throw in with them. He said he was in San Antonio the day before they left and he saw that feller walking around as big as life!"

"I'll be damned and double damned!" Tom exclaimed. "And I was thinking all along . . . Why that dirty, double-dealing sonofabitch! Hey, what are you doing now?"

"He told me last night to grab his saddlebags if he went down," Fergie said, going over to Biscuit's horse—which waited patiently beside them—and untying the laces holding the pouches in place. "I figure I might as well take him up on it!"

He tossed the saddlebags over his own horse's withers and mounted up. Tom stared at him for a moment, shaking his head in wonder, and then leaped into his own saddle.

Rawley, Frenchy, Coleman and Red Shirt had ridden ahead after the horses. Fergie and Tom spurred after them, a hundred yards in front of the closest Indian, and rapidly drew away from their pursuers. A thin line of jogging figures on either side reminded them that they were not yet out of trouble, however.

"You keep your eyes peeled for the trail that Apache told you about," Tom yelled over at his nephew.

"We going to take it?"

"You're mighty right we are! But first I'm going to shoot me an old soldier friend!"

"Godamighty, don't go up against him, Uncle Tom! He's liable to pull one of them hideout guns and get you before you know it!"

Fergie fumbled through Biscuit's saddlebags as he rode. He first found a leather pouch that had a heavy feel to it; he stuffed it into the front of his shirt. Reaching into the second pouch, his hand closed around a pistol. There was nothing else in the bags and he flung them aside, keeping his grip on the pistol.

Darting a look over his shoulder, back to where Biscuit lay, he saw a blood-chilling sight. Already the barelegged figures were closing upon the body; as he watched, horrified, he saw one of them raise a heavy cudgel and bring it down on the limp form. Fergie twisted his face back to the front. Tom was riding furiously toward the remuda, veering to the left, where he had last seen Rawley. The horses had come upon an animal trail and were in a region of scanty grass; consequently they raised a tall cloud of dust and only dim figures could be seen in the tan fog.

As Fergie closed upon the remuda he saw Rawley dropping back from the group. The man appeared from the right side of the crowd of horses, directly opposite from where he had been earlier, and he began edging over toward Tom as he rode. Fergie was far enough to the rear to catch a clear look at the man as he dropped behind the others and moved over to come at his uncle from the rear. He saw the man reach into his open coat and bring out a pistol as he rode.

Fergie tried to shout a warning but could not get a sound out of his throat. He dug his spurs into his horse and quickly moved closer to the man. Suddenly, with no conscious effort on his part, the pistol in his hand began barking. He fired twice, hitting Rawley both times. The man dropped his pistol and went over, driven forward and to the side of his horse by the pair of .44-caliber bullets. Rawley slipped from the saddle but his left foot caught in the stirrup and held. The horse, spooked by the unfamiliar weight dragging at its side, veered off slightly to the right.

"He was getting ready to throw down on you!" Fergie yelled out as his uncle turned back and emerged out of the cloud of dust. "He was coming around from the other side, and I got him, I got him myself! He had a gun out and he was fixing to go right up your back, honest he was!"

"Well, I ain't too surprised at that," Tom said, reining in

beside his nephew for a moment. "He must have figured that Biscuit let it out while he was kicking off; old Biscuit never could keep anything to hisself for very long. All right, don't you fret none about it; he'd have done the same to you and with a lot less reason!"

They rode toward the others, who had stopped upon hearing the firing. Tom approached Coleman and Frenchy warily, pistol in hand but held down at his side.

"Fergie shot him; he was going for my back," Tom explained. "He must have figured that Biscuit had spilled the beans about that dodge you fellers run on us back in San Antonio. And you know what? He was right!"

"Tom, I didn't much like the idea," Frenchy said, "but by the time they got back to camp that night it was all settled. It didn't seem like it would be no more trouble to go along with it than it would be if I started raising sand. I don't reckon it would do much good to say I wish it hadn't turned out thisaway."

"No, I don't reckon it'd change much at all," Tom agreed.

"Red Shirt says the trail down into the canyon's about a half a mile or so up ahead there," Coleman said. "Come on, let's head for it!"

"I reckon not," Tom replied. "Me and Fergie, we're making a run for it. You can have our part of what you find."

Fergie had been looking ahead, scouring the landscape for a glimpse of the trail Red Shirt had mentioned. His eye caught a faint scar, barely lighter than the surrounding patches of grass; the indentation pointed off to the right, or to the northeast. He looked back and found Red Shirt looking at him. The Apache nodded solemnly and raised a hand, almost as though he were bestowing a blessing upon the youth.

"I think that's the trail over yonder, Uncle Tom!"

"All right, that's for us," Tom replied. "You boys staying here? Well, I hope you make it and that ain't no lie!"

"Damn you anyway," Coleman fumed, whirling his horse about sharply. "We'll find the silver ourselves!"

He clattered off toward the rim of the canyon, followed

closely by Red Shirt. Frenchy hesitated a moment, obviously split almost in two with indecision, but then he spurred after Coleman without a backward glance.

"Come on, boy," Tom muttered, "let's get after it now!"

Tom led Fergie away at a different angle. Up ahead and to the right they saw a small group of Indians standing over a dark, shapeless object; their clubs rose and fell feverishly. Rawley's horse was galloping back from the group, stirrups flapping emptily.

"Let's grab that horse!" Tom shouted. "Bax hid his poke in them saddlebags, I bet he did!"

They headed the horse toward the dim trail Fergie had seen and quickly caught up. Fergie herded the horse loosely as Tom bent over to slash at the laces holding the pouches in place behind the cantle. As soon as he had freed the saddle-bags and had swung them over to his own horse he reached down to unfasten the cinch; the saddle slipped off and went tumbling as the horse surged ahead of them.

Three Indians ran toward them as they swept into the trail Fergie had marked, but Tom snapped off a warning shot that brought them skidding to a halt. They contented themselves with flinging a stone each at them and then shouting angrily. The trail led down a gentle slope and disappeared into a thick stand of junipers ahead.

"Watch it," Tom called out. "Them woods might be alive with Indians!"

They met no Indians in the junipers but Fergie caught a glimpse of something that gave him a vast pleasure.

"That's Mosca!" he yelled, pointing to a rangy brown geld-ing which was darting along the trail in front of them. "Here, boy, come on up!"

They rode at a gallop until the trail began twisting back and forth in its descent from the mesa. Mosca, a six-year-old that Fergie had raised from birth, fell into place in front of them as did a bay mare Coleman had bought in Parral. Those two, together with Rawley's horse, gave them three extras, and suddenly their situation looked much brighter. They did not see a single trace of Indians, though they kept up a brisk pace until noon, at which time they shifted their saddles to spare horses, paused to take a few bites of food from their saddlebags and then rode on.

The trail wound down into lower regions, and by nightfall they found themselves in a rough, broken country. Tom kept them going, always pushing north, and they found a twisting, racing creek beside a peak which bent over at the top, giving it a certain moonlike quality. Fergie pointed it out to his uncle, explaining that Red Shirt had described it to him, and he also mentioned the old Apache's advice about following the creek.

"You know, I think we just might have done it," Tom said, heaving a great sigh as they unsaddled and began fashioning makeshift hobbles from their ropes. "By God, it sure looked grim there for a while, though!"

"I wonder how them others is doing?"

"It'd be better not to wonder," Tom said. "They'll be mighty damned lucky if they saw the sun go down tonight, much less see it come up tomorrow morning. I'd a sight rather be here than there, and I don't care how much silver was down in that canyon!"

Fergie rolled up in his blankets at once and fell asleep. The excitement of the day had drained his energy and once they seemed out of danger his very bones turned into jelly.

"What was them places that old Apache told you about?" Tom asked as they saddled up the next morning.

"Uh, Casas Grandes was one," Fergie replied. "And the other one was, uh, Janos or something like that. I hadn't never heard of neither one of them."

"Me neither. But if they're up thataway," Tom said, looking toward the northeast, "they've got to be closer to Texas than where we are now. Godamighty, boy, I feel almost like a new man, knowing there ain't no sheriff on the lookout for me. And then there's this, too."

He nodded down at Rawley's saddlebags. It had been too dark to investigate their contents the night before and he had been too exhausted to care; the pouches had a heavy, comforting feel and that was enough to reassure him.

"Yes, and here's the poke I got out of . . . out of Biscuit's saddlebags," Fergie added, reaching into his own saddlebags for the sack he had put there. "You know something? That's all he had in them, that and the pistol I found."

"It ain't much for a man to die with," Tom mused. "Well, you want to count it all up now or wait a while?"

"I don't care," Fergie said, but then he added, "Let's get moving again, huh?"

"Fine with me. We won't go no faster, knowing how much is in there, so I guess it don't matter much."

Tom opened Rawley's saddlebags and began sorting out the sacks of coins into roughly equal piles. They stowed the sacks away and mounted up. The sun was well up by the time they rode off from their camp.

"I don't reckon that old Indian said anything about how far it was to one of them towns, did he?" Tom asked as they got under way.

"No, not a word. I hope it ain't too far, though—I didn't think nothing about it last night but we might be hurting for food pretty soon."

"We'll get by as long as we got us some water and this creek, it don't look like it's going to peter out any time soon."

"I guess so. Well, even at that I reckon we're a sight better off than them others."

"You're mighty right we are," Tom agreed. "We might get an ache in the gut before we get to where we're going, but we'll get there!"